CHILDREN OF THE SUN

CHILDREN
OF THE
SUN

Harry Allen

Troubador Publishing Ltd
Unit E2 Airfield Business Park,
Harrison Road, Market Harborough,
Leicestershire LE16 7UL
Tel: 0116 279 2299
Email: books@troubador.co.uk
Web: www.troubador.co.uk/matador

ISBN 978 1805140 498

British Library Cataloguing in Publication Data.
A catalogue record for this book is available from the British Library.

Typeset in 11pt Minion by Troubador Publishing Ltd, Leicester, UK

Matador is an imprint of Troubador Publishing Ltd

To M&D
with love and thanks

ONE

*A*bove the gate to the stadium someone had painted the word *'traitors'* on a piece of board. The paint had run, streaming in thin red lines through the date – March 16th, Year of *Juche* 105.

She jumped down from the cart, the wind flicking her long black hair into her face, and pushed her way past the crowd heading towards the stadium. She took the harness and stroked the soft flank of the ox, letting it warm her. "Thanks for the ride."

It snorted in reply.

"Seo," called her father. "You go in with your mother. I'll take the cart around and tether up at the side."

"Yes, Dad." She stepped back and took a deep breath. Every second brought her closer to the event that the whole town had been waiting for, since the *Immiban* had walked from apartment to apartment, checking that all the first-timers, like her, would be there.

"Seo…" From his seat behind the oxen her father beckoned to her with his right index finger. A saw in the logging factory had claimed the tip just below his nail, and ever since she could remember she had found the slow, jerking movement hypnotic. She walked towards him and he placed his hand on her cheek. "Stay close to your mother and just remember what I told you earlier." He leaned in close and kissed her on the forehead. "Don't be afraid."

"I'm not afraid…"

But her lie got lost in the clatter of the cart as it pulled away, revealing her mother standing on the other side. She walked up to Seo and straightened the collar on her coat, brushing at the grey patches that pot-marked the front. Seo tugged at the sleeve and her mother tutted.

"I should have taken those down."

"You've already taken them down twice. I don't think there is any more material," said Seo.

"There's always a little bit more."

Her mother's best coat, at least a size too big, hung off her narrow shoulders; her yellow hat, kept in a box in the cupboard for special occasions, had frayed around the edges, leaving it looking frail and gnawed. She straightened it slightly, took Seo's hand and they joined the rest of the town as it moved through the gates.

Even in the twilight the spots of red paint that had dripped to the ground shone bright against the grey. Seo looked away, coughing as the smell of an old wood fire caught on the breeze and lodged in her throat. The grey walls of the stadium grew larger with every step, the last rays of the sun clinging to the top like fingers slowly losing their grip. Fear snatched at her and she flinched, squeezing her mother's hand, feeling the bones under her thin sack gloves. She tried to remember the new song she had been rehearsing, something to distract her, but the tune wouldn't come, the notes a jumble in her mind.

"Are you all right, Seo?" whispered her mother, pulling her daughter close. "Don't worry, you're old enough now, you can't stay at home for these things anymore. Remember what your father said."

Seo took a breath, brushing her hair away from her eyes, resenting the fear, trying to force it away. Hadn't she taken the hit from the soldier when she cut the rice queue, and would have the scar on her forehead for life? Dodged being volunteered for the rice harvest? Taken shortcuts through the farms more often than she could remember? Who else could say that? Come on, she thought, you can do this. But the fear crept back, crawling up her stomach and crouching inside her chest, and she realised it wasn't what she would see behind the stadium gates, but who it might be that scared her the most.

A memory formed in her mind of sitting on the floor in an old man's apartment, savouring every last crumb of a *Dalgona* biscuit, feeling the warmth from a coal-fired heater – please don't let it be Old Man Park.

Around her she recognised friends and neighbours, no one looking at her, no one talking. She spotted Nari standing with her father and half raised her hand to say hello, hoping for the comfort of a friend, knowing how much easier it would be if she could take her hand. But Nari looked straight ahead and Seo knew she couldn't delay the moment any longer. She turned and faced the far end of the pitch.

The prisoners stood on a platform tied to poles by three lengths of rope: one across the chest, another across the waist and one around the ankles. The relief that Old Man Park wasn't among them forced out an audible sigh. She tried again to get Nari's attention, knowing she would be sharing the relief, but Nari had obviously been given the same instructions she had, and stood completely still. She looked across the dust of the pitch and the crumbling stands around her, scanning the silent figures as they stared at the platform, but she couldn't see any sign of Min. She wondered how he felt, if the same fear ate away at him. A part of her hoped it did: if Min was afraid, then there was no shame in her being as well.

"Head up." Her father stood next to her. "Remember what I said."

Don't look sad. Don't talk. Don't look away.

She tried to force her eyes to rest on a spot just above the middle prisoner's head, but however hard she tried her gaze kept dropping to the figures on the platform, their clothes torn, their hair matted and filthy. She didn't recognise them, but she would have seen them, she was sure, walking in a street, singing at a party rally, trading something outside their apartment block. She had seen bodies before, several times – the Corpse Division were always busy, especially in winter – but she had never seen anyone die, watch their life leave them.

Clouds swallowed what was left of the day, bringing a dark drizzle that stuck to clothes and peppered the dust with black spots. Seo wiped her hand across her face, smearing the cold damp across her forehead, and watched as Mrs Lim, the Immiban, walked onto the platform, one hand holding a megaphone, the other raised in greeting. She wore thick, black-rimmed glasses that seemed to cover half her face, and even from a distance Seo could see her magnified eyes.

She wore a simple black skirt and coat, without a patch or mark on them. She always has nice clothes, thought Seo, nicer than anybody else. Mrs Lim stopped in the middle of the platform, lowered her hand and stroked the badge on her lapel, a portrait of the Great Commander and the Dear Leader. A rustle of movement drifted across the stadium as everyone did the same.

"Comrades!" She paused, allowing the echo of the megaphone to ricochet out of the stadium. "Since The Great Commander first drove out the American imperialists, their puppet government in the South has tried to weaken the will of our people. To make us turn from the ways of *Juche* and add our nation to their empire." She lowered the megaphone, taking in the crowd, before raising it again. "We will resist!"

"We will resist!" The shout of the stadium rocked Seo on her feet. She felt her father's hand on her back and straightened, keeping her eyes fixed on Mrs Lim.

"As you are aware, there have been several arrests recently and I am delighted to be joined by Colonel Nam of the Ministry of State Security, who has been instrumental in tracking down the traitors lurking in our community." She gestured to the side of the platform and Seo saw a man dressed in a dark grey suit standing motionless, his hands behind his back. The crowd applauded, but he made no gesture of acknowledgement and stared out across the stadium, the breeze ruffling his silver hair. He looked too young to have hair that colour, his eyebrows too black, and something about his stillness unnerved Seo. She turned her attention back to the *Immiban*.

Mrs Lim waited for the applause to fade before speaking again. "As your *Immiban*, the Party Representative, it is my duty to catalogue the crimes of the traitors you see before you." She coughed and sniffed before moving to the nearest stake. "Prisoner 2771: possession and viewing of imperialist propaganda in the form of printed matter with the intent of distribution."

Seo had heard about the propaganda the Americans kept smuggling into her country: books, magazines, sometimes even films, all lies designed to trick people into thinking life would be better under the rule of the imperialists. She had heard the whispers about them: machines in walls that gave you money, more food than you could eat, a car in every home. There had been times when she had wished she could see one of the magazines, catch a glimpse of a film, deeply curious about the fantasies the Americans tempted them with. But the sight of Prisoner 2771, his head hanging limp, lank hair forming a shroud over his face, drove away any such thoughts.

On the platform, Mrs Lim lingered for a moment, as if expecting some form of response, but the prisoner said nothing and she moved on to the middle stake. "Prisoner 2772: illegal movement between towns with the intent of defecting." Again, the prisoner made no response, but this time Mrs Lim did not wait, moving quickly, almost eagerly, to the last stake. Here she paused, staring at the woman, shaking her head in what seemed to be disbelief or sadness. The prisoner looked up and a startled murmur rippled through the crowd. Mrs Lim stepped forward and raised her megaphone.

"I hear your distress, comrades. Know that mine is far greater. As the *Immiban*, I am faced with many difficult scenarios, but none as difficult as today. I know you recognise prisoner 2773. Her husband was one of the cornerstones of our community, a farmer who died during the Arduous March against the famine imposed by the imperialist blockade of our nation, and she is my cousin through marriage." She put emphasis on the last words, *through marriage*, glancing in the direction of Colonel Nam as she did so. "Prisoner 2773 has been found guilty of hoarding three kilos of rice. All food must be distributed directly to our armed forces. Military first!"

The crowd responded, "Military first! Military first!"

Seo mouthed the words, trying to force out some sound with them. She knew the prisoner, had met her at party meetings when she'd talked of the bravery and sacrifice of her husband. Seo suddenly remembered the clawing emptiness in her own stomach, of how her mother weighed out each gram of rice from the jar. Strength began to return to her legs as she thought of the woman stuffing her face in her basement, laughing at the rest of the town. Her voice slowly returned, gaining power with each chant: "Military first!"

Mrs Lim called for silence and the crowd quietened. "Thank you, comrades, I know you appreciate the gravity of the crime. But rest assured, your farms are safe. I shall personally be taking control of the land to ensure that this cannot happen again."

Seo cheered, her fist in the air, hypnotised by the chants of the crowd.

Mrs Lim signalled for silence again and brought the megaphone up to her lips, but before she could speak another voice took her place.

"Liar."

Seo looked around, shocked that anyone would dare speak to the *Immiban* in this way.

"Liar."

The word had come from the stage. Prisoner 2273 strained against her ropes, thrusting her body towards Mrs Lim. "Liar! There is no rice there. There is no rice at all. The soldiers take everything, they—"

At the edge of the platform, Colonel Nam raised his hand, a movement so sudden after his total stillness that Seo flinched. A dark figure stepped in front of prisoner 2273, cutting off her words. She struggled for a while, thrashing against her ropes, before falling still. The figure moved away, back to his position behind the stakes, and Seo saw there were four of them, all soldiers, their black uniforms, boots and dark glasses merging them with the shadows. Prisoner 2273 fell silent, her body shuddering, face turned upwards, red froth squeezing its way between the sides of her mouth and the plastic ball that filled it. Seo looked at Colonel Nam, stunned by how effortlessly he had commanded the soldiers. He smoothed the parting in his hair, now dulled to grey in the dusk, and for a moment his eyes met Seo's, his hand coming to a sudden halt. She tried to look away but somehow his stare held her in place, cold creeping down her back, as if he had run his finger down her spine. He blinked and looked away, his hand coming to rest at his side as he resumed his former pose.

Seo took her father's arm, desperate for him to say they could go, that it was over. He placed his hand on her shoulder, looking straight ahead. Seo forced herself to do the same.

Mrs Lim began to speak again, reminding the crowd of the great debt they owed the leaders who had defeated the imperialists and kept them safe from colonisation, but Seo no longer listened. She could not take her eyes away from Prisoner 2273, as the reality of what was about to happen slowly grew in front of her. She had been angry at the thought of her keeping rice, but the sight of the battered body on the stage just brought guilt at how loudly she had shouted. She wanted to run, to hide in the trees on the hill with Min and Nari until the wind had blown it all from her mind.

A spotlight came on with a sound like someone slamming their palm down on a metal table. Seo winced under its glare and turned her head. At the far end of the stadium the light shone on portraits of the Great Commander, the Dear Leader and, slightly below them, the Great Successor, who now carried on the struggle that his grandfather and father had started.

She felt her father's hand on her shoulder again and turned back towards the platform.

Don't look sad. Don't talk. Don't look away.

The soldiers formed a line in front of the prisoners and raised their rifles.

Her father's hand gripped her tighter. *Don't look away.*

The first shots blew apart the ropes on the prisoner's chests in a grey and red haze. They slouched forward, heads bowed. The second blew away the ropes on their waist and they slumped to the ground, the last set of ropes holding them in a kneeling position, bowing to the portraits of the leaders of the Party.

Seo felt the world slipping away and forced herself to breathe in, taking long, slow lungfuls of air. When her vision became clear again the soldiers stood behind the stakes, rifles at their side, as if they had never moved. Colonel Nam had vanished.

"Comrades!" Mrs Lim was speaking again. "Let us never lose faith. Let us never give up our struggle. Remember, the spies of the South and the enemies of our people are everywhere. They could be standing among us now, standing next to any one of you!" She paused, allowing the words to settle over the crowd. "And let us now remind ourselves of the precious land we are so privileged to share."

The crowd began to sing as one: 'No Country Without You', a song of praise written for the Dear Leader and now sung for his son, the Great Successor.

> *…our country cannot exist without you. You are the sun of our lives.*

A nudge from her father told her she must join in. She clenched her fists, forcing out the words, singing as hard as she could.

> *…without you there would be no us! Without you, no motherland!*

The song ended, bringing complete silence to the stadium. Seo moved with the crowd towards the exit, her feet making no noise as she stepped over the spots of red paint under the archway. Ahead of her a man jerked forward in a silent sneeze, and she knocked the palm of her hand against her ear, trying to get rid of the low humming that seemed to have robbed the world of sound. Her hands shook; fear and shock starting to overwhelm her. Someone caught her arm and she screamed, the sound of her own voice breaking the silence, flooding her head with the noise of the departing crowd.

"It's all right, Seo," shouted her mother, putting her arm around her shoulders. "This way. Stay with me."

Seo allowed herself to be led away from the crowds, down the road to where she saw her father already sitting in the cart.

"Come on, you two." His voice had never sounded so welcoming.

The drizzle had stopped and the clouds moved on, leaving a clear, star-specked sky. Seo sat in the front of the cart, her head nestled against her father as he drove the ox cart up the hill, the night wind rasping in her ears.

"Are you all right, Seo?" asked her mother from the back, resting a hand on her shoulder. "Do you want to talk?"

Seo shook her head. "I'm all right. I don't want to talk about it."

Her mother squeezed her shoulder. "I didn't either the first time I saw an execution. But remember, we must trust the Party. They know what is best."

They rode past others walking back towards town, and her father called out to them, offering them a lift. Seo was worried someone would say yes, but they all refused, perhaps lost in their own thoughts, and the further from the stadium they went, the safer Seo felt – away from Mrs Lim and her megaphone, the soldiers and their guns – until she felt she could ask the question that had been growing steadily louder in her mind.

"Dad…?"

"Yes, Seo?"

"Is that what they did to Old Man Park?"

Her father didn't answer at first and she heard her mother shifting in her seat.

"You still think about him?" asked her father. "And it's Mr Park to you."

"We shouldn't talk about him," said her mother, learning forward from the back. "Especially not on night like this."

"It's all right." Her father looked down at Seo. "I don't think they executed him, no. A Crow came for him and that's all there is to say." He gave a half laugh. "Except that he was a good man."

"But he must have done something wrong to be taken away," said Seo. "Committed a crime?" Her father turned to her again, and Seo nearly jumped, startled by the anger in his eyes.

"That's what they tell us, isn't it?"

"That's enough!" said her mother. "I'm not listening to any more. Seo, why don't you sing a song for us? You missed your practice today. It will help drive away this cold."

Seo wanted to talk to her father more but didn't seem to have the spirit to argue, as if the executions had bled it out of her. She still remembered sitting on the small rug in Mr Park's apartment with Nari and Min, a black and white picture flickering on his television screen. He had been one of the few people in town to own a TV and he welcomed them over once a week to watch. He had been gone a year, but Seo still remembered the smile on his face when he opened the door and the smell of the freshly baked *Dalgona*. No one knew where he got the sugar from, and Seo never asked. On days with no electricity they would sit in the kitchen as he told them stories of the war against the Americans or of films he had seen, the three friends nibbling their biscuits, trying to make them last as long as they could.

It had always confused her that the Crow had come for him because she didn't understand how someone like that could have been an enemy of the state. Her father's reply had confused her even more. Everyone else would simply have agreed he must have done something wrong.

"Come on, Seo," said her mother, tapping her on the shoulder. "Let's hear that lovely voice of yours."

"I don't want to, Mum. There's too many people, it's embarrassing."

Her father cleared his throat. "You have been given a great gift, Seo. It is only right you share it with the people. Besides, your mother is right – it will help with the cold."

Seo closed her eyes for a second, willing herself not to argue, hoping Min and Nari weren't close by and the light too faint to see her by. She took a breath and began to sing, softly at first, but her voice gained strength as her confidence grew and the comfort of the lyrics drove the executions to the back of her mind. "*We are the nation of the free.*"

Behind her mother began to hum along.

"*Strong and proud as can be.*"

They passed a family on the road and the man took up the song, urging the others to do the same. Somewhere in the darkness someone else joined in, and soon Seo could hear voices up and down the hill, all singing together.

"*And we have nothing to envy, nothing to envy, in the People's Republic of North Korea!*"

TWO

Seo gripped the letter in both hands, holding it against her chest, knowing it was the most precious object she had ever possessed. The executions had replayed in her mind for the last two days, tainting her thoughts and lurking in her dreams, but the words she had just read had driven every shout, every sound and shadow away. Nothing mattered now but the letter.

Ignoring the rain, she ran across the street from the Party's office to the station, taking the steps two at a time, her face beginning to ache from her smile. Inside, the electricity had gone and she slowed a little, worried about tripping over a beggar or a body in the gloom.

"Sister," whispered a voice in the shadows. "Pity me."

She held up her hand to show she had nothing and hurried through, down the steps and through the alley on the other side. She came out onto the main road just as the Information Van drove past and skidded to a halt, silently cursing the van but knowing running would be seen as suspicious. She tucked the letter under her coat and walked on, her chest heaving with every breath.

"*Brothers, sisters, we march together towards the final victory against the imperialist aggressors.*" The words crackled out of the speakers on the roof of the van, some lost occasionally in static. "*As... nation we... endure... onwards. Long live the Great Successor!*"

She raised her hand, fist clenched, like the few others that walked the street. "Long live the Great Successor!" The van moved on, creeping along the empty road. Come on, move it, thought Seo, but she watched until it was far from view, its words lost in the rain, before starting to run. The road took her past the building where she had had her audition and she waved to the grey concrete walls, remembering the three faces that had stared at her from behind the thin metal table and the fear that had gripped her as they asked her to begin her song. It had been so long she had almost given up hope of ever hearing from them. She stretched out her arms, her face turned towards the tumbling rain. "Thank you!"

Following the road home would take too long, so she had two choices: cutting through the back of the Community Rice Distribution Centre or the Municipal Allotment. The welts left from the security guard's cane at the distribution centre still hurt when she sat, but more importantly if he caught her it would mean a delay. She picked the allotment. It was off limits and she would be in trouble if the caretaker caught her, but he was old and she was fast. She sprinted down the alleyway and squeezed herself between the gate and its post, ducking under the rusting chain and padlock. She got halfway across the small patch of mud, minding the few weeds that had squirmed their way to the top, before she heard the all-too-familiar voice.

"Ra Eun Seo! I see you trampling the crops. This is the third time this week. I will tell your father. It's once too often!"

She ran the last few metres, throwing herself up onto the wall.

"Come back, you sparrow!"

"Sorry, can't stop," she shouted, clambering down the other side and away towards home.

Outside her apartment block residents squatted under tarpaulins, resting their backs against the crumbling plaster, trying to sell whatever they had or could find: a light bulb, string, small cakes made of rice (everyone knew they had sawdust in them), tree bark for people who couldn't walk the hills to strip it themselves, a plastic doll, a chicken leg.

"Eun Seo! Welcome, sister. Come and see what I have today."

"No time, Shin. Not today." She rushed past, taking the concrete stairs to the third floor two at a time. The padlock that secured her apartment door hung open; someone was home.

"Mum! Mum!"

"In here, Seo. Don't shout, please."

Seo ran through the living room, knocking against her father's chair. The broken leg gave way and it toppled to the floor.

"Seo!"

Seo burst into the bathroom, her head brushing against the sanitary towels hung up to dry.

"What is all this noise?" said her mother. "Did you knock over your dad's chair?"

Seo held out the letter, her hand trembling a little, a trickle of sweat running down her cheek.

Her mother looked at it for a moment then snatched it out of her hand. "You better not be in trouble at school again."

Seo just smiled as her mother turned the envelope over in her hands, straightening a little as she saw the Party's stamp. She ripped it open, read it, looked at Seo, then read it again.

A light seemed to grow in her mother's eyes; her grey-streaked hair took on a new sheen, the smile giving her face new life. "Oh, Seo..." Her mum's voice was little more than a whisper. She looked at her daughter for a moment then, with a cry, grabbed her in a hug. "You clever girl. You extraordinary girl."

"Things will be different now, won't they? Everything will change. We're going to live in the capital and have rice every day and maybe they'll even give Dad a car and we can drive to the countryside and there'll be hot water and a big apartment and everything will—"

Her mother pressed her finger to Seo's lips. "Shhh..." She led her daughter out of the bathroom back to the living room, stopping under the portrait of the Great Commander that hung on the far wall, turning to Seo and resting her hands on her shoulders. "We must be sensible, Seo," said her mother. "Remember that this is all thanks to the Party and the Great Successor." She kept her back as straight as she could, her eyes suddenly dull and distant, as they were whenever she spoke about the leaders or the Party. "Individual success is not important; only the motherland matters. We must not be seen to be thinking only of ourselves. Don't tell anyone yet."

Seo opened her mouth to protest, but her mother got there first. "We must speak to your dad. Do you understand?"

"Can't I tell Nari at least?"

"Seo! We must speak to your father first. We must do things the correct way."

She knew better than to argue; her mother wouldn't budge on anything that involved the Party or the leaders, and she took a deep breath, trying to contain her frustration. "All right."

"Do you promise?"

She nodded. "I promise."

Her mother pulled her close and kissed her on the forehead. "Please try to understand. You've brought us the best news this family has ever had and I couldn't be more proud of you. But this is a great honour that you've been given and you must be a responsible citizen now."

"But I've waited so long. I'd begun to think I wouldn't hear from them at all. And now I can't say anything."

"Don't worry – when we can, we'll celebrate like we never have before, I promise you that. Until then, I'll keep the letter safe." She gently folded the letter, placing it in the patched pocket of her apron. "Now, hard though it will be, you must try and forget this for a while. Put all that energy to some use. Do your chores. And when you've finished you can go foraging." She kissed her again and walked back to the bathroom.

Seo looked down at her now-empty hands and took a deep breath. The urge to lean out of the window and shout the news at the top of her voice threatened to be too much. But she knew her mum was right. She mustn't think of herself, not this time; it was too important.

In the kitchen she found the rag that served as a duster and busied herself with her chores, trying to force her mind away from the letter. She concentrated hard. First the cabinets: three plastic plates, three cups and a muddle of chopsticks, two cans without labels, and a plastic tub full of tree bark. The cabinet with the door held the kimchi jar and the rice sack. A single corner of paint clung to the front and she dusted around it carefully. Had it been yellow or orange? The bucket for the well stood next to the sink – plenty left. She dusted a cobweb away from the water taps. In the capital the taps would work…

She sat back on her heels, not trying to fight it anymore. She had been chosen to sing the solo songs at the Festival of the Sun in Pyongyang, the annual celebration to mark the birthday of the Great Commander. The final solo marked the climax of the celebration and she had read the letter ten times before she really believed it had happened. It was an honour that would change her life completely, might even mean a permanent move to the capital to take her place among the elite of the country, her family counted among the Loyal Class, those closest to the Party and the leaders. She'd heard that people who lived in Pyongyang could shortlist three things they wanted to do for a living. If the Party agreed and they could demonstrate enough skill, they could spend the rest of their lives doing something they wanted. Seo let the feeling build, her hands beginning to tremble. She let the duster fall to the floor and jumped to her feet, screaming out the words in her mind: *I'm going to be a singer!*

• • •

Seo looked up as the sun sliced through the clouds, the warmth spreading from her face across her body. She stopped and closed her eyes, arms outstretched, not wanting to waste a single ray.

"Hurry up, Seo," shouted Nari.

She opened her eyes and looked up the hill. Nari had already made it to the treeline and Sung Min must already be in the woods.

"Coming!" she called, then picked up her bucket and jogged up the hill."Where did you get your energy from?" asked Nari.

"We had rice for lunch. Thirty grams boiled with a chicken bone and a spoonful of kimchi on top."

Nari's eyes widened in surprise. "What are you celebrating?"

Seo looked away, trying not to smile. "Mum was feeling generous, that's all."

"I could have done with that. Only cabbage for me so far. But I won't get anything else unless this bucket's full."

"Let's go then."

The trees at the edge of the wood had been stripped of their bark long before, their trunks standing weak and starved, naked branches reaching out to the town below. A few tufts of grass still grew at the base of the trunks, but they were inedible, and Seo knew they would have to go much further in to find the bark and shrubs they needed.

"I hope we won't have to go too far…"

"There's green up ahead," said Seo. "Anyway, Min would have found something. He always does."

"I know. It's not normal." Nari dropped her voice to a whisper, looking around her as she spoke, as if checking for the *Immiban*. "I think he's really a sorcerer."

"You can't say that!" Seo laughed.

"He finds things where everyone else has failed. How is that possible?" She walked towards Seo, her back hunched, her hands tightened into claws, dropping her voice to a cackle. "You better watch out, he'll turn you into rice fertiliser!"

Seo cowered, holding her hands up in defence. "No! Anything but that!"

They let their laughter run its course, Nari bending down and tightening the string that kept the sole of her boot attached. "Shout out for the little wizard then. He's got to be somewhere near."

"Min! Where are you?"

She waited a moment. The sun had gone, and she ran her hands down the front of her jacket, checking it was tied properly.

"Over here!"

They followed Min's voice through the graveyard of trees to a steep rise, Seo calling out again and Min's reply confirming they were in the right spot.

"Great," said Nari. "We're going to have to climb. I'll get my trousers dirty."

Nari's trousers were already dirty, marked with deep stains and patches, like Seo's, like everybody's. Yet, somehow, she still managed to look smarter than all the others: her hair always shone, she didn't have a pimple on her entire face and her lips formed an almost perfect bow. She could be dressed in rags and you might believe she'd just got back from a ball in Pyongyang.

Seo swept back her own, slightly greasy hair, feeling the scar on her forehead, the awkward size of her ears as she tucked her hair behind them. I have my voice, she thought, Nari has her looks and I have my singing voice. For a moment the urge to tell Nari about her solo performance at the Festival of the Sun almost got the better of her, but she stopped herself. Her father hadn't returned to the flat before she left, so the promise of silence she gave her mother still held.

"Are you coming?" asked Nari.

"Why are you in such a rush today?"

They had to crawl up, dragging their buckets with them, the stones digging into their knees. Sung Min stood in a small grove at the other side, his bucket already half full of bark and grasses, all good bulk for soups and stews.

"How do you do it!" shouted Nari, slowly navigating her way down the slope with careful steps. Seo half ran, half slid past her, landing at the bottom in a cloud of leaves.

"Nice one, Min," said Seo. Min smiled and pushed his glasses back up his nose. The frames had been repaired so often they were more tape than plastic, with a crack that ran the entire diagonal of the right lens.

"There should be plenty for all three of us," he said.

He was shorter than everyone else their age, and his head looked too big for his body, like a child's doll. His father had died in the Arduous March against starvation and everyone said his head looked that way because he hadn't had enough to eat when he was young. But he could fix anything, find anything, and Seo couldn't remember a time they hadn't been friends.

It took them an hour to fill their buckets. Min vanished for about ten minutes, returning with two handfuls of wild-mushrooms. Once they had all calmed down and the girls had stopped shouting his praises, they divided them up and placed them carefully in the buckets.

"I'm done," said Nari, sitting down with her back to the slope.

Seo looked at her bucket. "Me too."

"There's still some room. If we go up a little further we can…" The girls stared at Min, cutting him off mid-sentence. "All right," he said, one hand up in submission. "I think we have enough."

He sat down opposite the girls, picking a blade of grass. For a while nobody spoke, then Min broke the silence.

"I saw you both at the stadium…"

Seo's stomach lurched and she glanced at Nari, who looked away, the colour draining from her face.

"I saw Nari," said Seo. "But I didn't see you."

"I was further back, near the portraits." They fell back into silence for a while, Nari prodding at the ground with a short stick, her hair covering her eyes. Seo wanted to talk about what had happened, how she had felt, but wasn't sure how to start. Min beat her to it.

"I keep going over it in my mind." Min looked at the trees while he spoke. "I think even up until the last minute, I wasn't sure what was going to happen. I think I was just so relieved it wasn't Mr Park."

"Me too," said Seo. "I felt sick going in. But my dad said they just took him away like we thought."

"I miss him," said Nari. "And his biscuits."

Seo nodded. "I never want to go back to the stadium. I felt sorry for them. I knew I shouldn't, but I couldn't help myself."

"My mum said that one of them was caught leaving the district without a pass, so that's why they thought he was trying to defect," said Min. "But maybe he was just trying to find food. He lived on the north side, behind the logging factory."

"Could have been looking for food," said Seo. "There's not much up there anymore."

The wind picked up, catching the smell of decay from the dead forest, circling it around the grove, forcing it into their lungs. Seo coughed and pulled her bucket closer.

"Do we have to talk about it?" said Nari. "It's over and we have to trust the Party. They did it for the right reasons."

Min and Seo answered in unison. "Of course they did. I would never doubt it." It was what they always said whenever they talked about the country or the Party. Seo couldn't remember when it had started, but they seemed to have come to the unspoken conclusion that if they announced their loyalty at the end it didn't matter what they had said before.

Getting back up the slope was hard with a full bucket, but they made it to the other side without losing a blade of grass. At the top, Seo bent down to tie her boot fastenings, leaving her bucket leaning against the trunk of a tree. Finished, she stooped to pick it up but stopped, staring down at the roots.

"Come on, Seo!" called Nari. "What are you doing?"

"Hang on a minute." Seo knelt down, pinching something between her thumb and finger, and pulled – the tip of a plastic bag appeared. Using both hands she wrenched it from the ground and fell backwards in a spray of earth and leaves.

Min held his glasses a little way from his eyes, peering at the bag. "What is that?"

"It's just garbage," said Nari.

"Shhh…" said Seo. "I don't think this is garbage. Something's wrapped up in here."

Nari and Min squatted down beside her as she slowly

unwrapped the plastic bag. Inside that was another, spotted with dirt and mulch. Seo unwrapped the second and a ball of newspaper fell out at her feet.

"Told you," said Nari.

Min picked up the ball, weighing it in his hands before ripping it open, revealing a small black box, about 20cm by 30cm.

"Told you," said Seo.

Nari ignored her. "What is it?"

Min studied it for a second before pulling a long silver antenna from the top. "It's a radio."

"No way!" Seo clapped her hands in delight. "We could trade that for loads of stuff."

"You see this?" Min pointed to the front, where four symbols had been placed in the bottom corner: 'SONY'. "Those are English writing characters. And they mean it's from Japan."

Seo took a deep breath. "Loads and *loads* of stuff…"

"We better hide it," said Nari. "Lots of people are going to want something like that." She stood and scanned the woods. They were alone. "Come on, let's get moving, Min." Nari turned to him, but he said nothing, staring at the back of the radio, his hands trembling.

"What is it, Min?" said Nari. "What's the matter?"

"I don't think we should try and trade this."

Seo stood. "What? Are you mad?"

"Quiet!" hissed Min. "Sit down. You too, Nari."

The two girls sat down next to him in a huddle, their heads almost touching as the trees groaned in the wind.

"Listen closely," said Min. "Whenever the government decides that someone can have a radio or a television each one issued has a lead seal on the back – Old Man Park's would have had one too – this tells you that it's approved by the Party. What it actually means is that it has been doctored to only receive North Korean programmes. It's a measure to protect us from American propaganda."

"So…?"

"This doesn't have a seal. Whoever hid it here has been listening to programmes from the South."

Seo brought her hand up to her mouth, staring at the radio. Nari let out a gasp and stood, spinning around, searching the trees for anyone who might be watching, before dropping down to her knees. "Bury it, bury it now," she said. "One of prisoners was doing something with propaganda right? This could be theirs…"

Min reached for the plastic, but Seo grabbed his hand, holding it tight.

"Just wait a minute. Let's think…" She breathed heavily, welcoming the mixture of fear and excitement crawling up her body. "Let's switch it on."

"Are you mad?" said Nari.

"There's no one here. Besides, all we've done is found a radio, and that's not illegal. Anyone would switch it on." Seo felt the excitement build inside her. "Come on, you've both heard the stories. If Min didn't know about the seal we would have done it already."

"This is not one of your stunts, Seo." Nari lowered her voice to a hiss. "This isn't taking a shortcut through the fields or tricking Mr Chi into thinking he didn't set any homework. This is real trouble. Did you keep your eyes shut at the stadium?"

"Oh, come on, it's nothing like that," said Seo. "We're

not stealing or selling propaganda. All we've done is found a radio and switched it on. That doesn't make us traitors."

"But this isn't an ordinary radio and we know we shouldn't."

Seo looked at Min. "What do you think?"

"We might hear the Americans."

Nari flicked her hand in front of Seo, with an expression on her face that screamed 'I told you'.

"And don't forget," continued Min, "that '*the chief outside force that stands in the way of our country's independent, peaceful reunification is US imperialism*'."

Seo stared at Min for a moment. "You memorised that?"

"Of course, it was homework. It's from the Great Commander's *On the Building of the Worker's Party of Korea, Part 4.*" Min blinked at her through his glasses. "You mean you didn't?"

"Never mind that," said Nari. "We've decided – bury it."

Min reached for the plastic bag then stopped, staring at the radio as if it was made of rice.

Nari poked him. "Come on, Min."

He kept his eyes on the radio. "I've always wanted to listen to a real radio."

"Me too," said Seo.

"Come on," said Nari. "Quickly."

"No one else has seen it and Seo's right, if we hadn't checked the seals we would have done it already." Min ran his finger slowly across the top of it. "It might not even work... I wonder if I could fix it...?"

Seo leaned forward, almost whispering in his ear. "I bet you could."

He took a deep breath. "I know a place we could go."

"You are both *insane!*"

• • •

Min led the way through the trees, the radio hidden under his jacket. Nari looked pale, her head jerking round at the slightest sound. Maybe the news she got that morning had gold-plated her confidence, but Seo couldn't share Nari's fear. Anyone would want to listen to a radio they'd found. Besides, they had their buckets, so no one would question what they were doing in the woods.

The trail stopped at the top of a small hill. The trees had thinned and the sky opened up above them. "We should be safe here," said Min. "No one ever comes; there's nothing to eat. The reception should be better too."

They knelt down on the ground in a circle. Nari slipped her arm through Seo's, holding it tight. Min pulled out the radio and extended the aerial before slipping off a small cover at the back. Two batteries fell into his hand. He held them up, rolling them between his fingers, before slipping them back inside and closing the cover. He looked at them and smiled.

"Ready?" he said.

Seo felt a sudden heat in her chest, her heart jerking once before resuming its rhythm, Nari's grip on her arm getting tighter.

The radio had two circular switches at the top above a small speaker. Min flicked the first one and the speaker began to hiss. It rose and fell as he moved the other switch, patiently rolling it back and forward with his thumb. But no matter how many times he did it, no other sound came.

Nari let out a long, slow breath, untangling her arm from Seo's. "Well, that's crap. No better than Old Man Park's TV."

"Shhh, let's give it a minute," said Seo, her excitement dissolving in the white noise. "Min?"

Min shook his head. "I don't think it works…"

Seo snatched it from his hands, her frustration building. "No one is going to bury a broken radio with two good batteries they could trade still inside. Who has that much food?" She stood, holding the radio above her head, swinging it from side to side.

Min grabbed her arm. "Sit down!"

"It's no good," said Nari. "Not even you could fix it, Min. Just take the batteries and throw it away before someone sees us."

Seo sat and slapped the ground with the palm of her hand.

"And turn it off," said Nari. "I hate that noise."

Seo pressed a button on the side, and the noise switched to a low crackle. She stared at it, holding it away from her. Min reached out and took it slowly, carefully, as if it might shatter at any moment. He moved the tuning switch and the speaker spat out a single word: "…*other*…"

Nari gasped, creeping forward on her knees, the crackle from the speaker returning. Min moved the tuner again and the voice faded back in, and held.

"…*eastbound traffic. And that's all from me. Now back to*…"

A woman's voice came on, but what she said didn't seem to make much sense to Seo: she wanted people to tell her what their favourite form of social media was and how often they used it. Seo looked at Min, hoping he might know what social media was, but his eyes stayed fixed on the radio, his mouth slightly open.

"…text me your answers. But only when it's safe to do so!"

Seo desperately wanted to know what a text was and why they could be so dangerous, but the woman moved on quickly and she didn't want to miss a word.

"…have you eaten anything this week you've never eaten before? Let me know for a chance to win. The weirder the better!"

It was a strange thing to ask, and the whole tone of her voice was nothing like the presenters on the state radio. It had to be from the South – propaganda trying to convince her they had more food than the North, but everyone knew they were starving; if it wasn't for food aid from the Party, the imperialists would have starved them all long ago. Then the proof came.

"…best-rated radio station in Seoul and South Korea…"

Next to her, Nari gave a muffled cry, her hand over her mouth. But Seo couldn't hold back her smile, the adrenaline rushing through her. They were doing what only a handful of people were allowed to do, listening to the forbidden.

The song started a little while later (after a man told them how his watch could measure his heartbeat). The presenter talked a little about 'blues' and a 'golden era', and names she had never heard before, then silence, followed by the song. From the first chords, bows sliding across strings, pulling the sound from the speaker and letting it free among the trees, Seo knew she had never heard anything like it before. She inched closer, unable to tear her eyes from the speaker, as if the music was something she could see. Then a woman started singing in tones from another world, the strange language wrapping her up and lifting her off the ground, until nothing existed but the song. She thought about the songs to the Party she had been so proud to sing, of the one she would sing at the Festival of the Sun, and how colourless and soulless they now seemed. And she knew that all she wanted to do, all she would ever want to do, was be able to sing like the woman from the radio.

Long after it had finished, they sat on the hill staring at the radio, the signal lost, replaced by the deep crackle and the occasional, semi-coherent word. The wind ruffled their hair, the trees around the clearing creaking as it passed and Seo knew something had changed in her: that there had been the world before the radio and now the world after it. When she spoke at last, telling the others that they must keep it, even Nari agreed.

THREE

The view from the hillside looked out across mottled apartment blocks towards grey paddy fields and the matchstick trees on the slopes. In the far distance a line of women washed clothes in a stream that ran by the railway tracks, their bodies just tiny silhouettes against the horizon. The sun sent slivers of light through the clouds, turning the surface of the stream into a ribbon of silver. But Seo looked straight through it all, her eyes filled with the buildings and streets of Pyongyang, the national stadium, the sound of a thousand hands clapping her performance. She dreamed about it often, both asleep and awake, but she never sang the song she had rehearsed; she sang the song from the radio, relishing the awe on the faces of the audience.

"I can't believe you didn't tell me," said Nari for the fifth time. She lay on her back staring at the clouds, chewing a stalk of wild grass. "I mean… it's me!"

Seo had given up trying to explain. Partly because she

had run out of ways to, but mostly because she knew, deep down, that Nari understood.

Mrs Kim had made the announcement, ending an agonising month for Seo. She had marched into her school flanked by two soldiers and Seo had felt the blood drain from her face as the classroom rocked and her mind filled with excuses: she had found the radio but was frightened to hand it in; she hadn't listened to it and never would; she... Her mind froze, unable to process any more thoughts except one, please don't faint, please don't faint, please don't...

But Mrs Kim's had not come to arrest her and her face had broken into a smile as she told them all about Seo's great honour of singing at the festival, reducing her teacher, Mr Chi, to tears. All the class had been there except Nari, so she had been the last to hear.

"Where have you been the last few days anyway?" said Seo, nudging her friend with her foot. "We could have talked sooner."

"I was on my way to school on Monday, but I got volunteered."

"Oh no... What duties?"

"Night-soil," said Nari, in a mixture of disgust and embarrassment. "They're starting to gather fertiliser to store over the winter."

Seo groaned. "That's the worst. I had three days of that last year. They didn't even give us tents to sleep in."

"I swear there are people who crap more than they eat."

Seo laughed.

"I guess there won't be night-soil duty in the capital, though..."

Seo turned her face away, trying to hide her smile. No,

she thought, I don't think there will be. They sat in silence for a moment, then she remembered the gift her teacher had given her.

"Look at this," said Seo, pulling a small lapel pin from her pocket. "Mr Chi gave it to me as a farewell present."

Nari sat up, the grass stalk dangling from her mouth. It was a miniature portrait of the Great Commander painted in enamel. It looked similar to dozens Seo had seen before, but slightly larger, the enamel brighter and the Great Commander's glowing smile clearer than she had ever seen on something so small.

"It's beautiful," said Nari.

"He said the Great Commander gave it to him himself..."

Nari snorted with laughter. "You can't believe what that old radish says."

Seo put the pin back in her pocket with a shrug, slightly hurt. "I believed him."

"Well, you'll be meeting the leaders yourself soon enough." Nari pulled the grass stalk out of her mouth and threw it away, not able to hide the envy in her voice. "You better not forget about us."

Seo shuffled up and put her arm around her. "How could I? Besides, you'll be coming to the performance."

"Really?" Nari sat up straight in an instant. "You can do that?"

"I'm the soloist," she said. "I'm allowed guests. My parents, obviously, but it should be no problem to get travel permits for you and Min."

When she had first started to talk about singing at the Festival of the Sun, it had sounded unreal to her, as if she was listening to someone else speaking. But slowly her confidence had grown and with it a love of the awe it inspired in others. "You know, I might even be able to get permits for your parents too."

Nari threw her arms around her. "You're the best. I was born to live in the capital..." She stood and flicked her hair back before curtsying to empty air. "Hello. My name is Yeo Nari. I'm the wife of a *very* important Party official. I'm on speaking terms with the Great Leader himself..."

Seo laughed. "You're crazy."

"...we're thinking of moving to Kijong-Dong when my husband retires."

"Now you're really dreaming!" Seo had never heard of anyone going to Kijong-Dong. The town had an almost mythical status, the perfect community, built on the border with the South to show them how successful the Great Commander's country had become. Seo allowed the thought of a visit grow in her mind but dismissed it with an audible 'tut'. She hadn't even got to Pyongyang yet. She left Nari with her daydreams and crawled on her hands and knees to Min, who sat struggling with the radio.

"How's it going?"

"No luck so far."

"Please make it work."

She listened to the radio every day, with the others if they could make it, or just on her own, longing to hear the song again, but they still hadn't played it. There had been others, some more familiar, but nothing affected her like the first one had. The propaganda stories gave some compensation, though. *Blossoms on the Moon* and *Hard Road Home* were their favourites and came on a few times a week, telling a chapter of the story at a time. At first she laughed, baffled and nervous, but soon found herself sucked into the world of cars and bars, hotels and restaurants, characters who owned their own homes, televisions in every room – the radio gave her whole new worlds.

"I don't think we're going to get anything today," said Min, pushing his battered glasses back up his nose.

"I don't understand. It worked fine in my room the other night."

"You shouldn't listen to it at home. Why do you always do things like that? Anyone could hear you."

"Nobody did. It's fine."

Min rolled his eyes. "Anyway, the signal has to come a long way; it won't always be clear. Lots of things can affect it, even the weather." He carried on in silence for a while, holding the speaker to his ear as he turned the tuning dial a millimetre at a time, listening for changes in the static.

Seo watched him, admiring his determination. He never gave up on anything, she thought, like when they went out foraging. People said it was luck that he managed to find so much, but Seo knew it was hard work, studying the areas where things grew, understanding the seasons. He didn't leave things to chance. Min reached up and scratched his cheek, before resuming his task. He's quite good-looking, too, she thought, despite his slightly odd head. A thought drifted into her mind, like a piece of notepaper caught on the breeze, but she brushed it away, unsure of what it meant.

"It's no good," said Min. "I can't get a signal."

"Let's keep on trying for a bit longer."

"It's getting dark, Seo," said Nari. "We should go."

"I just want to listen to it one more time."

Min pushed the aerial down and switched it off. "Forget it, Seo. If there's no signal, there's nothing I can do."

Seo turned away, trying to hide her frustration. She left for Pyongyang in two days and this would probably be her last chance to hear the voice that still sung so clearly in her head, or just one more of those extraordinary stories. At home in her room, she had to keep the volume so low she could barely hear a thing.

"What are going to do with it when Seo's away?" said Nari.

Min shrugged. "Keep it hidden until she gets back, I suppose."

"We'll just keep it hidden in my room then," said Seo. "No one will find it there."

"I've enjoyed listening to it, but I'm a bit relieved we're taking a break," said Nari. "We've taken such a risk…" She stopped suddenly, staring at Seo, as if a sudden thought had physically hit her. "You better not take it to Pyongyang. You would be in so much trouble."

"I wouldn't do that."

"I know what you're like…"

"I'm not stupid. Don't worry, I won't take it."

"Please don't," said Nari, a hint of fear in her voice.

"Relax, Nari. I promise."

"Come on," said Min, "let's go. Seo will hide it in her room. It's been safe there so far."

Seo slipped her arm through Nari's. "You worry too much."

They walked together down the hill to the town, the radio wrapped in rags and hidden under grass in Seo's foraging bucket. They walked carefully, the light almost gone, the remains of the day lying like a memory on the horizon.

"It's going to be a bit dull around here now," said Min, sending a stone bounding down the road with a flick of his shoe. "No radio and no Seo."

"Hey! I'm still here," said Nari, punching him lightly on the arm.

"Thank the Leader for that. I'd go crazy on my own."

They passed the old cinema, its windows boarded up and the door chained. Seo had never seen a film there, but her dad had told her about the films he used to watch as a boy, a new one every month, about the Korean victories over the Japanese and the Americans. I bet the cinemas are still open in Pyongyang, she thought.

"What's that?" Nari stopped, pointing up the road.

"I can't see anything," said Seo.

"A light..." said Nari. "There it is!"

In the distance Seo caught a flash of white light, then another.

"It's a car," said Min. "Must be a Party official or an army officer."

Seo watched the lights as they drew closer, fading in and out as the vehicle dipped over the hills, getting closer, until she could make out the shape, framed in its own lights. Her heart froze. "Black Crow!"

"Get out of sight!" shouted Min.

Seo vaulted the wall in front of the cinema and crouched down, Nari landing next to her, clinging to her arm. Seo pushed her bucket with the radio into the shadows just as the Black Crow skidded to a halt outside the apartment block on the other side of the road. They heard the doors slam shut and the sounds of the soldiers' boots as they thundered onto the stairs, then silence. Seo counted slowly in her head, trying to guess which floor they must have reached. The count reached five just as the noise of splintering wood echoed across the road and a woman started screaming. Seo covered her ears but couldn't keep out the shouts and thuds, the screams and tears as the soldiers dragged the occupants of the flat on the fifth floor down the stairs and out into the street. Seo turned her head and found a hole where one of the bricks had fallen out. They had come for Mr and Mrs Son. Seo knew their daughter, Su Jun, from school, but she hadn't spoken to her much. She watched as the soldiers bundled them into the back of the lorry, the ones they called the Black Crows. There was only one destination – all the Crows flew to the prison camps. Sometimes people came back, but mostly they didn't.

The door of the Crow slamming silenced Mrs Son's screams. Seo adjusted her position slightly, trying to see more of the apartment and the Crow. A man stepped into view, his black shoes shining against the dust of the road, not a strand of his white hair out of place. Seo recognised him at once, the colonel from the Ministry of State Security who had been at the executions. She pulled her head back, looking at the others and bringing a finger to her lips as the sound of Colonel Nam's footsteps came closer. He stopped, and a cigarette butt flew over the wall above their heads, falling just below Seo's feet, the deep-red tip staring at her through the thickening dark. Nari's finger's dug into her arm and a tear of sweat trickled down her cheek. She lifted her eyes, half expecting to see Nam staring down at her, but a voice called out and his footsteps faded away towards the Crow. A door opened and shut, the tyres skidded once before holding, and the noise of the engine slowly faded into the distance.

They sat in silence, Nari muffling her sobs in her sleeve, Seo listening to her heart as it regained its usual rhythm. Gradually they heard voices from the apartments, the Sons' neighbours asking the same question that filled Seo's mind: what had they done?

"Come on," said Min. "We shouldn't hang around in case people start asking questions about where we've been."

They climbed back over the wall, Seo helping Nari, her bucket with the radio suddenly almost too heavy to hold. They kept to the side, hiding in the shadows, Seo suddenly desperate to be home and the radio safe in the hole in the wall. She glanced back. People had begun to gather outside the apartment block, their voices carrying through the night, the tracks of the Crow dissolving in the night wind.

Days Since Arrest:	5
Time:	09:45
Location:	Interview Room 4
Subject:	Jane Doe
Age:	Unknown
Origin:	Unknown
Medical Condition:	Evidence of severe physical trauma
	Evidence of Post-Traumatic Stress Disorder
	Unwillingness or inability to speak

Interviewing Officer: Kim Soo Jung

X – *Do you remember me? I'm Kim Soo Jung.*
NO RESPONSE.

X – *Are you afraid to speak?*

NO RESPONSE.

X – *I'd love for you to talk to me. Why don't you tell me something about yourself? Anything you like.*

NO RESPONSE.

X – *I'm forty-two. How old are you?*

NO RESPONSE.

X – *Won't you even tell me your age?*

NO RESPONSE.

X – *Why don't you tell me about things you like to do?*
Did you ever have a hobby, something you were good
at?

SUBJECT BEGINS TO SHAKE AND CRY. MEDICAL
OFFICER CALLED.

Interview Terminated: 09:47

FOUR

"Again!" Madam Lim struck the floor with her cane, the sound cutting through Seo's singing, forcing her to break off with a flinch. "The transition to the final note must be flawless. You are holding on to too much air. Your first instinct when you finish must be to *breathe*. If you don't use all the air, you can never achieve the full power of your voice." She turned, her hands behind her back, her cane tapping the rhythm against her shoes. "Again!"

Days consisted of twelve hours of rehearsal. Some of these were in groups with other girls who would be singing chorally, but Seo spent half the day in an old gymnasium with Madam Lim, working on the songs for the solo performances she would sing in front of the Great Successor. Her footsteps had cleared a path in the dust to the single chair and table in the centre where Madam Lim waited for her each morning. A criss-cross of lines was still visible on the floor, court markings from the sports that had been played there. At either end, two basketball hoops hung rusting from the walls, a few strings of netting still clinging to the rims.

"The acoustics here are just what we need," Madam Lim had told her on her first rehearsal. "We can stay dry but still have some sense of singing outside. But you will have to give me your best effort every day."

They had got through the first two songs without much difficulty, but no matter what Seo did, no matter how hard she tried, Madam Lim was never satisfied with her performance of the third. Time after time she heard the shout of 'Again!', the crack of the cane and started once more at the beginning. When the exhaustion took hold, when she had to fight back the tears, she wondered if she would ever finish, if she was condemned to stand in the empty hall singing the same song for eternity.

"Am I keeping you from something, Miss Ra? Is the final song of the Festival of the Sun not enough to keep your attention?"

"Sorry." Seo readied herself and began the first verse, concentrating all her thoughts on the music, the words and her voice.

"No, no, no! You are straining." The cane again. "You are all technique and no *feeling*. You must believe what you sing." She stared at Seo for a moment, then gestured for her to sit down. "Come, you must sit for a while, rest your voice."

Seo sat down heavily on the chair while Madam Lim poured her a cup of the herbal brew she kept in a flask. Despite the bitter taste, Seo drank it eagerly, relishing every drop as it slipped down, bringing immediate relief to her swollen throat.

Madam Lim waited for her to finish, then took the cup and placed it on the table.

"I have trained many singers, and all have done well. But there was one, some time ago now. She sang for the Dear Leader, shortly before his death. The final note she sang…" She paused, lost in the memory for a while. "If you had heard it, you wouldn't have believed such a note was possible."

"I'm trying," said Seo.

Madam Lim tutted, dismissing Seo's response with a flick of her hand. "The note itself was not important. You could have made it, any of a hundred girls could have. It was what was *behind* the note that made all the difference. People believed what she sang, could feel the emotion; it moved many to tears. Most people just sing words and music. That girl sang the truth."

Seo nodded, unsure if she really understood.

"Close your eyes."

Seo did as she was told.

"I want you to picture all the people in your life you have loved."

An image of her mother cooking in the kitchen burst into life behind her eyes. Seo heard herself gasp. She hadn't spoken to her since she had arrived in Pyongyang and suddenly ached to see her, to hug her, to share a simple bowl of soup at the table. How long had it been? Three weeks?

The day she left her town behind it seemed as if everyone she knew had gathered at the train station to see her off: all her classmates, people she knew from self-criticism and volunteer work in the neighbourhood. Her teacher, Mr Chi, stood tall, his hair the colour of winter clouds, his jacket almost slipping off his shoulders.

No one without a travel permit could take the stairs to the platform, not even her parents, so they hugged on the bottom step, her mother trying to hide her watery eyes under the brim of her hat.

Seo looked about at the crowd and found Min and Nari standing near the back, their hands raised. They had said their goodbyes the night before, but she was glad they had come. Mrs Kim walked up and shook her hand. She even managed a smile that looked like she meant it.

"Go on now," said her father. "You'll miss your train."

A mixture of anxiety and excitement gripped her heart as Seo reached up and kissed him on the cheek. "Goodbye, Dad."

The departure scene dissolved, turning to images of Min and Nari collecting grass and bark in the woods. Seo thought about the two hot meals a day of rice with chicken or fish she ate in the canteen. She had almost forgotten what it was like to feel hungry. The third image was the strongest: her father, walking towards her on the main road through the town, a smile on his face and a flower in his hand.

"Can you see them?"

Seo nodded.

"Come, stand up." Madam Park took Seo's hand and helped her out of the chair. Seo moved to speak, but Madam Park pressed a finger to her lips. "Say nothing. Hold those feelings in your heart as you sing. Now, again!"

Seo inhaled deeply, shifted the weight on her feet, shut her eyes and began to sing:

Can you see the blood on the leaves of the trees?
Can you smell the smoke as it rides on the breeze?

A flash of colour passed across her eyes – a glimpse of a

forest, the trees speckled with blood. The next lines seemed to come effortlessly, as if she had known every lyric, every note, all her life:

All we have to do is call our general's name,
Our Great Commander of undying fame.

The images paraded in front of her eyes, faint but familiar, like memories from another life. She saw the Great Commander, young and poor, tending the graves of the rich. She saw warplanes fly overhead and heard the sound of their engines. The Great Commander threw down his shovel and ran to the aid of his people. Seo inhaled and started the next verse, and with the words came a crescendo of emotion: anger, hope, pride, love – love for the peasant boy who defied the rich, who drove back the Japanese and crushed the Americans. And with the emotion, she felt her singing fly out of the hall, through the town and out onto the wind.

He crushed all our enemies, set our people free,
He will rule Korea forever, the sun of liberty.

She reached the last lines, holding the final note for longer than she thought possible, before falling backwards into her chair and letting the tears flow freely.

Slowly the room came back into focus. Seo wiped her eyes and took a trembling breath. She hadn't heard Madam Lim's shout, or the crack of the cane on the floor, and became worried that she had not been paying attention, had somehow missed it, and would be in trouble.

Madam Lim stood very still in front of her, her head tilted to one side. Outside a bird made a single call. She pulled up her chair and sat in front of Seo, taking her hand in hers. "How do you feel?" she asked.

Seo struggled to catch her breath. "I… I'm not sure."

Madam Lim leaned in closer. "You felt love for our Great Commander. You have always known *of* love for him, but through the song, through our rehearsals over these past three weeks, you now *feel* love for him. This is why I make you work so hard, to repeat the song so many times, because through the work we can see the truth."

"My teacher at school used to say the Great Commander was the father of all of us. I don't think I ever really knew what that meant until today."

Madam Lim stood. "That is good." She smiled, her eyes lighting up. "That is very good. For both of us." She placed her hand on Seo's shoulder. "That is enough for today. You have worked well. In fact…" Madam Lim paused, her cane upright in her hand, "you deserve a day off."

"Oh, thank you!" Seo let herself slump back in her chair, her legs stretched out in front of her, her arms dangling over the side.

"I have organised a trip for you, something to help clear your mind. Tomorrow a bus will pick you up and take you on a tour of the capital, finishing with the most important public building in Pyongyang, the Victorious Fatherland Liberation Memorial Museum."

Seo sprang up, her excitement beating her exhaustion. "Really? Tomorrow?"

"Tomorrow. All the other singers will go. And dress smartly. There may be another surprise for you as well…"

• • •

Seo checked the ribbon on her *Joseon-ot*, making it sure it flowed from the white blouse down to the full red skirt, smoothing any wrinkles the journey had made. It had been a surprise present from Madam Lim, left hanging in her wardrobe, and had confused her at first. Girls only wore *Joseon-ot* for weddings or traditional festivals, and it seemed a strange thing to wear to a museum, but all the other girls on the bus wore one, so she assumed it highlighted how important the place was.

One of the girls shouted with excitement, and Seo leant forward to see. The Victorious Fatherland Liberation Memorial Museum stood behind a giant bronze statue of a soldier holding a flag, reaching back with his left hand as he leant forward, urging his comrades to follow. The flag seemed to flutter in the breeze, and he looked ready to leap from the podium and rush into battle. All the girls were on their feet and moving towards the door before the bus had even stopped, their usual reserve collapsing in the excitement.

A female army officer waited to greet them, her hands behind her back and a smile on her face. The breeze tugged at her cap, ruffling the tufts of hair poking out from the side, and she tucked them back under as she waited for the girls to assemble.

"Welcome to the most significant monument to our Great Commander's victory over the American imperialists. I am one of the curators of the museum and your guide for today. Please follow me."

Seo had always known the Americans had started the war; she had been told it since she could remember. But walking through the museum's marbled halls, past photographs of captured Americans, display cases full of uniforms, weapons, mess tins, she felt the truth build inside her, just as she had felt love for the Great Commander through the song she would sing at his birthday. She felt the truth that everything she hadn't had as a child, every meal that hadn't been enough, the Arduous March through the famine that left so many dead and the permanent state of fear at the threat of war – the Americans caused all these things. Only the power of her leaders held them at bay, the only leaders in the world with the courage to defy the American pigs. And now she had become part of that struggle, a member of the Loyal Class, living in the capital in her private room, never hungry, playing her part in supporting the great leaders.

She could have stayed in the museum all day, breathing in the wonder of it all and her new role in the world. When the curator announced the tour was over, she almost asked if they could go around again, but she knew that would be rude. So she bit her tongue and started planning how to persuade Madam Lim to organise another trip.

They stopped outside a pair of doors and it took Seo a few moments to realise the curator had gone. A man stood in front of them dressed in a dark suit and white shirt. He silently mouthed the numbers as he counted the number of girls, his head bobbing as he kept track. Seo glanced around her, unsure of why the curator had left and why this man felt the need to count them. Finished, he turned and opened the doors.

The sky had cleared and the sunlight flooded the area in front of the museum, forcing Seo to drop her eyes for a moment. When she raised them again the plaza she arrived

50

at earlier that morning had vanished, replaced by the biggest crowd of people she had ever seen. The man gestured for them to follow and they moved towards the crowd, Seo struggling to understand what was happening.

The crowd had been arranged behind barriers in a large V shape across the plaza, with the bronze statue of a soldier urging his men into battle at the centre. The man led the girls towards the crowd, two others flanking them, and Seo knew if she looked behind her she would see the one at the back. They took up a position in front of the statue facing the road, the only section that didn't have any barriers. Seo looked at the man, hoping for some sign of explanation, but he moved away without a word. Around her the crowd stood silent. Some carried flags, limp in the breezeless day, held up in front of them as if they were unsure what they were for. Seo thought of the crowd at the stadium, waiting for the charges to be read out, and a shiver rippled across her body. Perhaps this is where they executed people in the capital.

A siren sounded in the distance, growing louder with each second, until it filled the plaza, rising and falling. Two motorbikes, riding exactly parallel, glided into sight followed by three black cars and another pair of bikes. The cavalcade slowed and stopped as one. A man in a black suit stepped out of the middle car, opened the rear door and, as if someone had pressed a button, the crowd erupted.

Seo had never heard anything as loud: screams, shouts, cheers; the noise of a thousand people gone berserk. She lifted her hands to cover her ears, then stopped, frozen by the sight in front of her. A man emerged out of the back of the car, leaning against the open door for support, his face stretched into a smile that seemed to reach around the side of his head. The Great Successor stretched out his arm, his hand waving back and forth at the crowd, turning to each side before walking towards the statue and Seo.

For a moment Seo thought she would faint, her head spinning with a rush of emotion, the song, the museum, Mr Chi's lessons, the roars of the crowd, everything converging into a sense of pure adoration. And before she knew what she was doing she began to run, tears streaming down her face, the other girls running with her, all desperate to be as close as they could to their beloved leader. The Great Successor's smile didn't falter for a second. He stopped, his arms outstretched, as if welcoming them all into an embrace. But before Seo could quite touch him she felt hands on her shoulders, guiding her around to the side. Camera flashes spotted her tear-clouded vision, but she could see the other girls, all being guided by the men in suits until they formed a semi-circle around him, all crying out as loudly as they could. "We love you! You are our sun, our protector!" Seo stretched out her hand, desperate to touch him, but she couldn't quite reach, and then, as quickly as he had arrived he moved back towards the car, waved at the crowd once more and was gone.

No one spoke on the way back, all the girls lost in their own thoughts. Seo's mind drifted to Min and Nari and how they would react if she told them who she had met. An image of Min's face lingered behind her eyes for a moment as she imagined him asking her to walk by the river with him, but she dismissed it. She was Loyal Class now and she would have to choose someone who wouldn't risk damaging that status.

She hardly noticed when they arrived, and one of the others had to give her a nudge before she slid out of her seat, off the bus and up the stairs to her room. At the beginning of the hall hung a mirror that Seo often stopped at to check her appearance in the morning. But that evening she could not look herself in the eye, and turned away, wiping at a small smudge on her blouse. But it wouldn't shift, a dark grey stain on brilliant white. She felt her eyes filling with tears again, but this time they weren't of love but of shame. Her mind filled with every time she had cut across the allotment, skipped her homework, questioned the wisdom of the Party or argued with her parents, and how petty and stupid they had been. She heard her mother's voice: *You must be a responsible citizen now.*

Yet all the trouble she had caused shrunk to nothing when she thought of the radio. She should never have even switched it on, never mind listened to it as often as she had. It had infected her, chipped away at her loyalty; the museum had shown her that. Every time she tried to keep the song she rehearsed with Madam Park in her head, the voice of the singer from the radio, the one she had heard the first time she had listened to it, kept whispering to her, humming the melody, knocking the song to the Great Commander out of tune. She had betrayed her leader's love, the leader she had been close enough to touch, and she knew the only way to get the voice out of her head, to make amends for her betrayal, was to smash the radio to pieces so neither she nor anybody else could ever listen to it again.

She turned, walking faster than usual but trying not to run. She knew the men she saw sometimes in the corridors weren't guests and she didn't want to arouse suspicion. The door to her room stood ajar, light spilling out into the grey corridor. She slowed down and sighed. Madam Lim would be there, waiting for her, another rehearsal before she went to bed, or perhaps she wanted to admire her in the *Joseon-ot* and hear the story of seeing the Great Successor. She pushed open the door, forcing a smile onto her face for Madam Lim, but it vanished in an instant. A man stood with his back to her, his white hair shining in the light, turning slowly as he she walked in, his face stopping her in her tracks.

"Good evening, Miss Ra," said Colonel Nam. "I am glad to see you back." He stood completely still, his thin face showing no expression.

"Good evening," she said, trying to sound as casual as possible. "Can I help you?"

Colonel Nam took a step to one side, revealing her small bedside table, the radio sitting on top. Seo quickly turned her face away, as if the sight of it had slapped her, trying not to believe what she had seen, the shock echoing through her body. She felt a movement behind her and strong hands pinned her arms to her sides. She wanted to call out, but no sound would come.

"I think you can help me with many things, Miss Ra. We have a lot to talk about."

FIVE

olonel Nam sat behind a desk typing, his hands lit by a lamp as he fired out words from the typewriter using a single finger from each hand. Occasionally he would get up, the metal chair grating across the concrete floor, and stare at the paper in front of him as if it had offended him in some way.

Seo sat some distance away under a twitching strip-light that sent flickering shadows across the floor. She knew the soldiers who had taken her from the hotel stood somewhere behind her, but she didn't dare turn to see. Fear held her, squeezed her in place, allowing only the intake of breath and a cold trickle of sweat down the side of her face.

Despite her friends' warnings, she had not been able to resist bringing the radio. The thought of not being able to listen to it had beaten her own doubts and fears, convincing herself it would be all right, that no one would look in the back of the second drawer of the chest in her room. No one had found it at home, so why should they here? And besides, she was a soloist, far too important for room searches.

She had lost track of how long she had been there. The ride from the hotel had only taken a few minutes, but her mind had been racing so fast she had paid no attention to where she was going. She tried to piece together a story in her head, something convincing about where she had found the radio, but she couldn't concentrate. Her left hand began to tremble, then her right, until her whole body shook, rattling the chair she sat in.

"Don't distress yourself, Miss Ra. I have nearly finished." There was no anger or threat in Nam's voice; it was soft, almost gentle, and Seo felt some of the fear slip away. She swallowed, the saliva squeezing down her dry throat.

"Thank you. I…" The blow came from behind, striking her on the side of the head and nearly knocking her to the ground. She sat up, rigid in her seat, gulping in air. She had had so many of those hits, from angry soldiers, from officials when she had been volunteering, that she knew not to make a sound or she would simply get another. Colonel Nam didn't make any sign that he had even noticed.

The clacking from the typewriter seemed to grow louder and Seo struggled to keep the room in focus. Eventually Nam stood, winding out the paper with a sound like a ratchet. He walked towards Seo, his eyes on the paper, and stopped in front of her, his hair glowing under the light, turning from white to silver.

"Do you know who I am? You may speak."

Seo nodded. "I saw you at the stadium when they—"

Nam cut her off with a wave of his hand. "I'm glad you

remember. Now: we need to discuss your radio. Remember, I am only seeking to confirm the truth. Do you understand?"

Seo nodded.

"Good – what is the truth? You may speak freely."

Seo couldn't speak. All the excuses and the stories she had been planning collided in her mind, splintering into unrecognisable segments.

"Let me help you," said Colonel Nam. "Someone brought the radio to you in your town when they visited from Pyongyang."

Seo recognised the trick immediately. She had heard it so many times at self-criticism sessions. He knew it was a lie. "No, I found the radio on the train. I saw it—"

"You are lying, Miss Ra. I will tell you once more: I only seek to confirm the truth."

He couldn't possibly know, she thought. What does he want to hear?

"It was in the hotel room; the last person there must have left it."

This time the blow knocked her clean off the chair and she lay, gasping, on the floor. She looked up and saw Nam standing motionless over her.

"I am a tolerant man, Miss Ra, but you are trying my patience." He straightened the chair. "Sit."

Seo pulled herself up and sat, the trembling returning to her body.

"Perhaps I have been unfair." The colonel paused, staring at Seo with unblinking eyes. "Perhaps you are under the illusion that you are in possession of the truth, is that it?" He nodded to himself. "Yes, I think that must be the problem." He walked to his desk and pulled out the chair, the legs scratching across the concrete, the sound drawing out the moment, turning seconds into minutes. He positioned the chair in front of her and sat down. "The truth does not belong to individuals, Miss Ra; it belongs to the Party, to its leaders. My job is to ensure that citizens understand the part they play in that truth. Some need to know that they are farmers or factory workers, but that is not an individual choice; it is one that is made for them to ensure the wider truth is upheld: we are under constant attack by the imperialists and their puppet government in the South and the only way we can stop the Korean people being enslaved is to adhere to the ways of *Juche* as written by the Great Commander." He paused and took a breath. "Do you know what *Juche* means?"

Seo looked away, her mind racing, unsure of how to answer.

"Any five-year-old could answer that question, Miss Ra."

The answer formed on her lips, but Seo couldn't muster the strength to say it.

"I cannot hear you."

"Self-reliance." Her words were barely a whisper.

"Good. You see? It is not difficult." He reached up and scratched his cheek, a movement so sudden Seo had to stifle a gasp.

"Self-reliance does not mean an individual's reliance on himself but the country's reliance on its leaders to show them the correct path to peace and prosperity. No one else can do this. No other country or government can help us, and no other leaders other than the ones we have can uphold this truth. Do you understand?"

Seo nodded. Behind her one of soldiers shuffled his feet.

"Just as the Korean people are one, so is the truth. It is

our joy, our solace and our armour. Outside influences are corrupt and lead people away from the truth. When this happens holes appear, leaks which the imperialist lies drip through. Too many holes and the drips become streams, then rivers, until the truth crumbles and is washed away, replaced with the evil lies of the Americans and their allies. And when the people realise they have been enslaved it will be too late. My job is to plug those holes when they appear, to keep the truth safe and, with it, the people. So you see, Miss Ra, the truth is not yours; it belongs to everyone." He stood, slowly straightening his back, and Seo thought she could hear each vertebrae in his spine sliding into place.

"Now. We will try again: what is the truth? You may speak freely."

"Someone gave me the radio when they visited the town."

"Yes, I know that. And? What is the truth?"

Seo's mind filled with ideas, words, sentences, but she didn't know in what order to put them.

"I am waiting…"

He must want to know what happened next. "I brought it on the train to—"

The side of her head erupted in pain with the slap and her vision blurred.

"Have you not been listening, Miss Ra? For the last time, what is the truth?"

Seo opened her mouth, tasting the blood from her nose as it trickled onto her tongue. Her mind screamed the answer at her, but the words came as a whisper. "I don't know."

The first emotion that Seo had seen rippled across Colonel Nam's eyes – surprise. "Good, Miss Ra. Perhaps there is some hope for you. Madam Lim, your singing instructor, brought the radio to your town and gave it to you after your audition for the Festival of the Sun." He stopped, looking at Seo, waiting.

A pain crept through her body, starting at her toes, and streaming through her head. Why would he say that? A blow from behind nearly knocked her from her seat again.

"Yes! Yes, it's true!"

"Good. The lies you heard on the radio corrupted your love for the leaders and you thought to share them with two of your friends…"

Seo's heart froze and she gasped for breath. He can't know who they are?

Colonel Nam walked to his desk and picked up his typed pages. "They are Rang Sung Min and Yeo Ji Nari."

Tears pooled in Seo's eyes and poured down her cheeks.

"I see your repentance," said Colonel Nam. "That is good. Remember your father loves you. Your country loves you."

The words of the song she had learned for the festival detonated in her mind, and she felt the love build inside her. What had she done? How could she have betrayed her country so badly? She saw no way out.

"Yes, that is true." She sobbed out the words, bringing her hands to her face. She barely heard the rest of the truth as Nam read it. She nodded and said yes when she knew she had to, and it was a moment before she realised he had finished speaking. She looked up to see him sitting across from her again, the pages he had typed resting on his lap.

"You have done well, Miss Ra. For yourself, your friends and the Party."

For the first time, Seo thought she felt some compassion in his voice. She looked at him through the tangle of her hair hanging in front of her eyes. "What will happen now?" No blow came from behind to knock her off the chair, and she straightened a little, wiping tears away from eyes.

"What always happens," said Colonel Nam, smoothing his hair with the palm of his hand. "The people will know the truth. Your instructor, Madam Lim, will be executed."

Seo couldn't muffle the cry that burst from her heart.

"It is not wise to show compassion for such people, Miss Ra. You do not know her history. She has already damaged her country, in ways you do not need to know, and was given a reprieve, a second chance to show her love for our country and its leaders. The people need to know that sometimes the corrupt cannot be reformed. It teaches vigilance. Lets them know that spies could be anywhere, maybe even living next door to them. Such examples must be shown regularly and publicly, or the people forget." He stood and walked to his desk. Taking an envelope, he slipped the typed pages inside and sealed it. "But I think you are more concerned with what is going to happen to you?"

Something landed with a thump next to her and she jumped, bringing her hand to her mouth.

"Your suitcase," said Colonel Nam. "All your possessions are inside, except the radio, of course. There is no place for you here in Pyongyang, but the Party always shows love to its people. You and your friends were corrupted by an agent of the Americans, but you are young and will be given a second chance to prove yourself to your country. Stand up."

Seo rose on shaking legs, relief and gratitude rushing through her. She tried to straighten her crumbled *Joseon-ot*, rubbing at the grime and blood that spattered it. Her relief vanished, replaced by a deep shame: shame at her actions, shame at herself, shame at the crumpled, stained dress that was a symbol of her country.

"Your transport is waiting downstairs," said the man. "Come. We must not be late."

He walked past her towards a door at the back of the room. Picking up her suitcase she followed, sensing the soldiers falling in behind her. She followed the man down a steep flight of stairs, her mind filled with the future. She would return to her town. It would be difficult at first, but she would do everything she could to make amends, even it took her the rest of her life.

The man opened a door at the bottom of the stairs and Seo walked out into the dawn. A large black truck squatted in front of her, its back doors open to darkness. Seo froze, trying to process what was happening. She felt strong hands grab her, pulling her towards the Crow.

"No, no, no!" she shouted. She felt herself being picked up and propelled forward, landing hard on the flatbed. "Please! I don't understand! You said I would have a second chance!"

"This is your second chance," said Nam. "Do not waste it."

Seo cried out again, but the crash of the doors slamming killed her words and she found herself in total darkness.

SIX

Seo sat, her hands flat on the bed of the truck, trying to steady herself against the rolls and jars. Occasionally, the truck hit a pothole so big there was nothing she could do, the pain shooting up her arms and spine. The only light came through a gap between the two doors, but it couldn't lift the dark, staying just of reach, a splinter of the world she had left behind.

Images of her parents came to her often: her father, smiling, beckoning to her with his half-finger, the other arm open in readiness for a hug; her mother, stern, shouting, tears of disappointment on her cheeks. She wished for some light, just enough to chase away the images before her heart broke. Colonel Nam had said she would have a second chance. Perhaps this was just the way they were sending her home? The doors would open and she would find herself outside her apartment block where Min and Nari would be waiting. The thought of her friends sent a new shard of pain though her body. She had told Nam they had listened to the radio as well. Perhaps they will never know, she thought, perhaps punishing me would be enough. But deep down she knew it wasn't true; there would be no surprises when the doors opened, that there could be only one destination for her – all Crows flew to the prison camps, each second, each jolt from the road bringing her closer. She lay down, curling herself up into a ball on the cold metal. It'll be all right, she kept telling herself, this was her second chance, they won't keep me locked up forever.

At some point Seo must have fallen asleep. She woke with a start as the truck bounced over an obstacle. She had no idea how long she had been travelling, but the splinter of light from the doors had gone. They slowed and she heard voices.

"One prisoner."

"Move on through."

The truck crawled along now, swerving a little from side to side. Seo had the sense of climbing a hill, the low gears of the truck whining with the strain. They stopped once more and she heard voices again, different this time, then the doors opened and a woman peered in.

"Out, out! Quickly!"

Seo scurried across the flatbed, dragging her suitcase, and climbed out of the truck.

"This way!"

She obeyed automatically, as she had at school or at party meetings, and found herself in a large floodlit courtyard surrounded on three sides by concrete walls. Razor wire twisted across the top of the walls, finishing in bundled coils on top of a wire mesh gate. Two other Crows squatted in the mud, their doors open, the drivers smoking in the cabins.

Seo followed the woman, clutching her suitcase to her chest, mud creeping up the sides of her shoes and oozing inside. The woman passed through a metal door and Seo found herself in a concrete room with metal tables stretching in a line through the middle, some empty, others with misshapen bundles covered by blankets. A leak from the roof struck the table she had stopped at, dripping out a metallic beat.

"Clothes," said the woman.

Seo looked at her, unsure of what to do.

"Clothes!" shouted the woman, and Seo dropped her suitcase and began to strip. She piled her *Joseon-ot* onto the table, followed by her shoes, and stood, one arm covering her bra, the other her knickers. A cold wind blew in, bringing a smell Seo didn't recognise – somewhere between stagnant water and rotting fruit.

The woman picked up Seo's dress, holding it out in front of her. Smiling, she put it back on the table along with the shoes, lifted up the suitcase and emptied it on the table. The hairbrush, the small stick of lipstick and Seo's bracelet she placed on top of the dress. The few remaining items she put back in and pushed the case towards Seo.

"These are your things," she said. "You may keep them with you." The woman bent down and pulled a bundle from under the table. "Put these on."

Seo stepped quickly into a pair of canvas trousers. The material scratched at her legs, falling an inch short of her ankles. The shirt was made of the same material and she pulled it on. Something crawled over the back of her neck and she shuddered, slapping it away.

The woman walked down the row of tables, stopping at the ones covered in sheets. She picked up the end and peered inside before moving on. At the fourth table she stopped and pulled the blanket clear off. Seo gasped, holding her hand to her mouth. She had seen bodies before, but never one so thin, so wasted, its mouth open as if trying to shout out. It wore the same canvas trousers and shirt that Seo had on, but the material had worn, exposing white skin stretched over ribs. The woman pulled off the boots and walked back towards Seo, dropping them at her feet.

"These should fit you."

Seo stared at the boots, unable to bring herself to touch them.

"Put them on!"

She sat down and clutched one of the boots. Turning her face away, she pulled it on, inching her foot inside. She pulled on the second and then turned away, dry retching onto the concrete.

"Not good enough?" said the woman. "You're lucky to have boots at all. Now get your bag and follow me."

Seo followed the woman to a door at the back of the room. The woman held the door open and Seo walked through, hearing it slam behind her, and she didn't need to turn to know she was alone. She stood in a large open space, a few lights blinking somewhere in the distance and the sound of a truck or lorry driving by out of sight. She had no idea what to do and clasped her bag to her, trying to find some comfort in its feel and smell. Two figures passed in front of her carrying a large pot on a pole balanced between them on their shoulders, their heads down, walking with short, shuffling steps. They wore the same uniform as Seo but made no sign that they had seen her, moving through the night in silence, and for a terrifying moment Seo thought they might be ghosts.

"What the hell are you doing?!" Seo turned towards the shout and saw two men in what looked like army uniforms striding towards her. One of them moved his hand towards the pistol on his hip. "Speak up, quickly!"

All of Seo's experience of authority kicked in and she bowed as low as she could. "Forgive me, sir, I have only just arrived. I do not know where to go."

The guards looked at each other in exasperation. "I thought no more scum was arriving today?"

"Another screw-up."

One of them grabbed Seo by the shoulder and pushed her forwards towards a sign nailed to a pole in the ground. "Stand here," he said. "Read that. Don't move."

Seo did as was told, her baggy clothes concealing the trembling that ran through her body. She started reading the sign, only just able to make out the words in the dark:

Camp 6
Redemption through Labour

<u>Rules</u>

1. **Do not attempt to escape.** *Any prisoner caught attempting to escape will be shot immediately.*
2. **Do not steal.** *Any prisoner found stealing or concealing food will be shot immediately.*
3. **Guards' orders must be followed without question.** *Any prisoner who disobeys an order will be shot immediately.*
4. **Prisoners must watch each other and report suspicious behaviour immediately.** *Carefully monitor the speech and conduct of others, and severely censure themselves and others at meetings of Ideological Struggle.*

5. **Prisoners must exceed their work quota.** *Prisoners who fail to meet their work quota will be considered to have disobeyed a guard.*
6. **Prisoners must repent their errors.** *Only through honest acceptance of past sins can a prisoner begin anew.*
7. **Prisoners must be truly grateful to the mercy of the state.** *The camp offers redemption through labour for those who have lost their way. Humility and gratitude must be shown at all times.*
8. **The guards are your teachers and redeemers.** *Anyone who attacks, harbours ill-will towards or disrespects a guard will be shot immediately.*
9. **Anyone who sees a fugitive or suspicious person must report them immediately.**
10. **Any prisoner who breaks or disregards the rules of the camp will be shot immediately.**

Only through obedience to the ten regulations of the camp and yielding to hard labour can prisoners cleanse themselves of their past sins.

The words began to blur in front of Seo's eyes, reducing to a few that seemed to shout at her in her mind: *guards, sins, labour, shot, repent.* She blinked, trying to focus, going back to rule one to try and read it again, but the words kept screaming at her: *repent, sins, work, labour, SHOT.*

"You!"

Seo turned, avoiding eye contact with the guard, keeping her head tilted slightly forward. "Yes, sir?"

"Follow me. Don't talk."

Seo did as she was told, following at a respectful distance

up a dirt track, the fall of her boots the only sound she could hear. A few lights peeked out of the dark, but she could not make out where they came from. Others seemed to be higher, and as they grew closer to one, she saw it was a watchtower, a guard looking out, his rifle and cigarette just visible. He took a drag and flicked the butt away, the red glow tumbling down before hitting the ground in a burst of tiny sparks. They passed other prisoners, but the guard paid them no attention, and they moved on, heads bowed, without a word. Seo's legs began to fail her, the muscles dissolving in fear, and she thought she wouldn't make it, that she would crumble onto the track never to get up. But somehow she managed to keep them moving, a single thought bringing her strength: *this won't be forever, this won't be forever, this won't...*

After what seemed about half an hour they stopped outside a rectangular concrete building, the wall dotted with boarded-up windows and a single wooden door in the centre. The guard opened the door; she stepped inside and he shut it again without a word. Prisoners lay in rows along the sides of the wall, all wearing the same grey uniform as Seo. They had formed groups with small gaps in between, like families suddenly thrust into the same space, trying to form the walls they used to have. Some seemed asleep, others murmuring to each other. One woman tied string around a boot, trying to keep a flapping sole in place. Three small fires burned in shallow holes in the floor, one at each end and the third in the middle, the smoke mixing with the smell of sweat, leaving soot marks on the concrete ceiling.

And there, squatting by the fire at the far end, their faces lit by the glow, sat Min and Nari.

Seo stood and watched them, unable to believe they were

there, squeezing her eyes shut before opening them again in case the light had played a trick. She glanced behind her, thinking for a second that she might go back out through the door. That would be disobeying a guard, but it might be better than facing the friends she had betrayed.

Someone bumped into her from behind and she stumbled forward a step. Min looked up from the fire and their eyes met. For a moment neither of them moved, then Min rose slowly to his feet and took a step forward.

"They sent you here too." He walked towards her, his hands clasped together across his chest. "I'm so sorry."

Seo couldn't speak, too stunned to even move, and for a moment she stood with her arms by her side, staring in front of her. Then Nari stood next to her, Min's hand touched her shoulder and she pulled them both close, giving in to the relief and the love.

SEVEN

They stood on a hill outside their building, the camp stretching out in front of them, brown and grey under a pewter sky. On the left, the road slipped down towards the entrance and Seo could just make out the sign declaring the rules of the camp. On the right she caught a glimpse of a black river running through trees, the leaves beginning to turn with autumn, the colours retreating up foothills towards low mountains. But it was the view to the front that held her attention: the camp stretched out to the horizon, and everywhere she looked there were people, hundreds of them, walking in lines down dirt tracks towards buildings and fields, never stopping, never talking, and the silence made her think again that they must be ghosts, wandering home from the night to sleep away the day.

The siren that had woken them slowly faded, rising and falling with increasing reluctance, as if someone had given up winding the handle. The side of Seo's body ached from the concrete floor they had slept on, the thin blanket hardly making any difference. Seo had folded it in half lengthways, lying down on one side, then pulling the other over. It didn't quite reach all the way, and no matter how many positions she tried a cold draught jabbed at whichever spot was exposed.

The other inmates had formed rows in single file. Seo had no idea where they were supposed to go, so they walked down past the lines of tattered uniforms to the end and formed a line of their own.

Seo nudged Nari. "Look at it," she whispered. "Did you know it was this big?"

"It looks bigger today. I've never seen so many people."

"Shh!" The voice came from the next line, and Seo and Nari stopped talking at once.

Two guards strode into sight followed by six prisoners. The guards stopped and the prisoners took up a position facing the others at the front of each line.

"Why are you here?" shouted one of the guards.

The response was instant and so loud Seo jumped. "We have betrayed the love of our leaders."

"What do you want?"

"Redemption through labour!"

The guard grunted, pulled out a cigarette and lit it, before turning away and chatting to his colleague.

One by one the prisoners who had arrived with the guards began calling out names, checking each reply off on a clipboard. None of them looked at Seo and her friends, and when they finished they led their lines away down the hill.

"Now what do we do?" whispered Nari. Min shrugged. The guards still stood talking and smoking. They didn't seem to have noticed the group who had been left behind.

Min put his hand up, holding it as high as he could. After a minute he coughed.

"What are you doing standing there?" One of the guards strode towards them, crushing his cigarette butt under his boot without breaking stride. He stood at the front of them, leaning forward slightly, his hands behind his back. His boots glowed with a deep polish and his uniform looked brand new, the Party badge shining on his lapel, despite the lack of sun.

"Forgive us, sir," said Min. "We arrived yesterday. We don't know where to go."

"Liars! You're trying to skip work! Do you know the penalty for that?" He chewed on his words, revealing a scattering of yellow and black teeth. Seo felt her legs begin to tremble and she breathed in ragged gasps.

"It's all right, Comrade Hwan," called the other guard. "If I'm not mistaken, they could only have arrived yesterday, probably only a couple of hours before me." He walked over, lifting his cap, revealing snow-white hair that sent a chill though Seo's heart. "Everyone deserves their chance to prove themselves."

Hwan took a step back, crossing his hands behind his back. "As you say, Colonel Nam."

Nam walked slowly past the three of them, looking them up and down, stopping next to Seo, his cap held under his arm. She kept looking straight ahead, not understanding why he was there, her head smarting with the punches from the guards in the interrogation room as if they had only happened minutes before.

"Do you recognise me?" asked Nam, his voice still and calm.

Seo nodded, unsure if she should speak.

"I cannot hear you?"

"I do. You are the one who showed me the truth." Seo tried to speak up, but she could only manage a whisper.

"Good. I am pleased to see you again, Miss Ra." He gestured to his colleague. "This is comrade Hwan, who is in charge of this section of the camp. His orders are law." Hwan lifted his chin, a glimmer of pride in his eyes. "Tell me, comrade Hwan: does this facility have a mine?"

"It does, sir."

"I think these three will make a fine contribution there. Please escort them." Nam smiled, an expression that seemed as out of place as the colour of his hair. He nodded his head slightly and replaced his cap, before walking away down the hill, whistling a tune Seo used to sing at school.

"Let's go!" shouted Hwan. "No talking."

Nari led the way down the slope, Seo in the middle and Min behind. Hwan walked alongside, his head nodding slightly with each step. He glanced at the three occasionally, muttering something inaudible. Anger seemed to surround him, reaching towards whatever was near, and Seo expected him to lash out at any moment. The fact that the man who had interrogated her was here frightened her, but she couldn't put her finger on why. She had confessed everything, so he shouldn't be a danger to her anymore. Besides, personnel were moved around regularly in her town, so perhaps it was just the same in Pyongyang. It might even be a promotion; Hwan certainly deferred to him.

Seo kept her eyes front, worried in case she was breathing too loudly, and with each step she told herself that she wouldn't be here for that long. She closed her eyes and tried to think of the song she would have learned for the festival, taking comfort in the lyrics. I won't mess this up, she thought,

I'll do everything I need to do to get out and will never betray my leaders again. And she knew from the conversation they'd had last night that Nari and Min would as well.

They had walked back to the fire where Min and Nari had been sitting and stood, silent for a while, each processing their own thoughts. Somewhere behind them someone had coughed, interrupting the flow of a half-whispered conversation. A cold breeze flicked Seo's face.

"What happens here?" she asked.

"We don't really know yet," said Nari. "They brought us straight here. It was empty when we arrived, then people started coming back. No one talked to us, though. They seem to have their own groups they stick to."

"Did you see the rules?"

Nari opened her mouth to answer, when Seo noticed a man not far away staring at them intently. He hadn't given them a glance before. They had managed to make their own space at the far end, but anyone could hear them unless they spoke in whispers. Seo put her hand on Nari's arm. "I saw them and will honour each one." She raised her voice a little, trying to make sure anyone else listening could hear. The man turned away and Seo looked at Nari, who understood immediately.

"And so will I."

Min stepped a bit closer, tightening their circle, forming a barrier between them and the rest. "Snitches?" he whispered.

Seo nodded. "Could be. We should be careful." The other two nodded. "Is this where we're going to sleep?"

"It must be," said Min. "But I don't think we're supposed to be all in here like this. You know, girls and boys. But I heard a few talking about a building collapsing, so I think that's why."

Seo nodded. "Food?"

"Nothing yet," said Nari. "But by the looks of everyone, I don't think it will be much when it does arrive."

"I couldn't eat now anyway," said Min.

Nari gave him a gentle push on the arm. "What are you talking about?"

Min looked down at his feet. "I need to tell you something." His voice cracked and Seo instinctively took his arm. Min looked up at her, then at Nari. "I've done something terrible."

Seo felt the tears creeping up under her eyelids. "I think I have too."

Nari just nodded, her face turned away.

They held hands and crouched down by the fire, the three friends taking turns to tell their stories. Min started, his voice breaking, head bowed so the flames from the fire couldn't throw light on his face. Mrs Kim, the *Immiban*, had come for him while he was at school and driven him to the local party headquarters. His 'truth' had been that Seo and Nari had introduced him to the radio, forcing him to listen, until he had been corrupted into listening willingly. Like Seo he had not seen his mother. Seo reached out her hand and held his, before telling them about coming back from the museum and her own confessions.

They had come for Nari at home. Mrs Kim arrived with two soldiers and a man in a suit. She had been allowed to pack a few personal possessions and to say goodbye to her parents, her mother crying almost uncontrollably, only the strength of her dad keeping her from falling apart. He had been calm and strong, reassuring Nari that he would get everything sorted out and that she mustn't worry. She had signed her confession at the Party headquarters and then been brought straight to the camp.

Seo stumbled on a rock and nearly lost her footing, forcing her concentration back from the night before. The slope led them down towards what Seo thought must have been the centre of the camp, dominated by a cluster of warehouses. She recognised the sounds of a sawmill from when she would visit her father at work before he lost his finger. She took a sharp breath, choking the sob that had formed in her throat. They rounded the corner of a two-storey building, its wall streaked black and grey, and Seo breathed in the unmistakable smell of coal. For a moment her heart lifted; the smell of coal had always meant warmth and comfort, a rare luxury on winter days.

The few trees and scrub that had lined the path began to thin, the ground under their feet becoming darker with each step. They rounded a corner of rock and came into a clearing in front of low cliff face, the ground black with coal dust that caught in Seo's throat, bringing the taste of burnt rock. Two sets of what looked like train tracks ran from a set of buffers in the centre of the clearing to an opening in the cliff face. As she watched a coal truck emerged from the hole, pushed by four prisoners, their clothes as black as their faces, the truck groaning forward a few steps as the prisoners pushed in unison. They reached the buffers and the prisoners began emptying the truck, shovelling the coal over the side of a ridge to an unseen destination below. One stopped, overcome with a convulsive cough.

Hwan turned to them, a smile on his face. "Welcome to your new home."

Seo reached inside her pocket and touched the lapel pin Mr Chi had given her the day Mrs Kim had announced she would sing in Pyongyang. She saw his face clearly, his thin neck craning out his suit, his hair the colour of winter clouds.

"Who is your father, Eun Seo?" he had asked, his voice kind but firm.

"The Great Commander. He is the sun and we are all his children."

"And where is he now?"

"His spirit lives forever in his mausoleum. He is our president for eternity."

He smiled at her, holding out his hand, the pin bright in his palm. "One of only a dozen made. He gave it to me himself."

"You met the Great Commander!"

He had tried to hide his smile but couldn't. "I fought the American pigs in our war of liberation and he heard of my service. After the war the marshal – that's what we called him in the army – said that for my service I could choose whatever I wished to do. I always thought that the children of the country were the most important thing we had, and I asked him if I could teach. He wanted to give me a university job, but I begged him to send me to the country where I could continue the work of the revolution and prepare the next generation of our citizens. He gave me this pin and sent me on my way."

"Have you stayed here all this time?"

"I have. And of all my students, no one has been given such an honour as you. You have helped to make all these years worthwhile." He placed his hand on her shoulder, as light as paper. "I am old now. Keep this pin, keep your father close to your heart, and one day you too can pass it on."

Seo clenched the pin tighter in her pocket, trying to draw strength from it and the man who had given it to her. "I will," she whispered. "I'm so sorry."

Interview 5

Days Since Arrest: 12
Time: 14:45
Location: Interview Room 4
Subject: Jane Doe
Age: Unknown
Origin: Unknown

Medical Condition: Evidence of severe physical
                       trauma
                       Evidence of Post-Traumatic
                       Stress Disorder
                       Unwillingness or inability to
                       speak

Interviewing Officer: Kim Soo Jung

X – *Good afternoon. It's nice to see you again. How are
you today?*

NO RESPONSE.

X – *Today I'd like to talk about where you are from. Can
you tell me that?*

NO RESPONSE.

X – *Is it nearby or far away?*

NO RESPONSE.
X – *Please don't be afraid. Perhaps you went to school?
Or perhaps you had a job?*

SUBJECT OPENS HER MOUTH IN WHAT APPEARS TO

BE AN ATTEMPT TO SPEAK.

X – *Did you have a job? Is that it? I've brought some paper and pencil. Perhaps you can write an answer down for me?*

SUBJECT TAKES THE PAPER AND WRITES.

X – *Let's see. You've written, "I will always meet the quota." I don't understand. What quota?*

SUBJECT BEGINS TO SHAKE AND CRY. MEDICAL OFFICER CALLED.

Interview Terminated: 14:57

EIGHT

Hwan shouted a command and a figure ran from the mouth of the mine, like a shadow detached from the deeper darkness. As he got closer Seo saw it was a prisoner, his face and clothes black with coal dust. He stopped in front of Hwan and bowed.

"New workers," said Hwan. "With the extra bodies, your quota just went up by half a ton."

The man visibly slumped. "Yes, sir."

"Get moving!" Hwan smirked, brushed a speck of dust from his uniform and walked back the way they had come.

The prisoner turned to the three friends. He looked quite old, several years older than Seo's father, his hair thin, coal dust filling the deep wrinkles in his face. He walked towards them with long, pigeon-toed strides, his shoulders bouncing, lighting a memory in her mind of an old man making tea while she sat on the floor with Nari and Min watching films on a hazy black and white TV.

"Half a ton!" shouted the man. "You sparrows couldn't pull a kilo. But I'm the supervisor here," he tapped a red strip of cloth tied to his arm, "and if the quota isn't met, none of us eat, and if I don't eat tonight I'm going to blame you. Do you understand?"

They all nodded.

"We always meet the quota! Do you understand!"

"Yes, sir!"

He took a step closer to Seo. "What are you staring at?"

Seo swallowed hard, unsure if she should say anything, but the words came out before she could make up her mind. "Mr Park?" Next to her Min straightened, taking a sharp intake of breath.

Nari took a step forward. "Old Man Park?"

Park seemed to shrink away from them, recognition sweeping across his face. "You three... is it...? You used to come..."

"You used to let us watch your television," said Min. "You used to make us tea."

Park nodded, all the anger gone from his voice. "I remember. How did you...?" But he didn't finish his sentence. He ran his hand down the front of his face; taking a deep breath, his body straightened and the anger returned to his voice. "It doesn't matter who you are! You're in here for crimes against the state and you'll work until you are released or you die. Follow me. No talking!"

Park led them towards the entrance of the mine.

"You walk down until you can't walk any further. The diggers bring the coal up from the face. You load it onto the trucks and push it up here. Unload it and take the truck back down. No talking, no resting. Get moving."

Seo looked up at him and saw, for an instant, the old man she had known in town, felt the warmth of the biscuit in her hands, before his face hardened again and the emotion in his eyes vanished. "Now!"

Min led the way down the shaft, following the tracks. Every few metres an electric light flickered on the wall, but the deeper they went the less effective they seemed to become, the light clinging to the walls, never fully penetrating the dark of the tunnel. Nari reached out and took Seo's hand. "Old Man Park turned into a bit of a dick."

"At least we know where he went."

The slope grew steeper and Min slipped, falling back and knocking into Seo, who fell back against Nari.

"Sorry!"

"Are you all right?"

"Fine."

Min picked himself up and they carried on. Seo's eyes began to sting, tears welling up, trying to wash out the dust, and she wiped them away with the back of her hand. Nari started to cough.

A tapping sound grew louder with every step, joined by another and another, building into the disjointed rhythm of dozens of picks hacking away at rock.

They turned a corner and nearly bumped into one of the coal trucks. Apart from the noise there was no sign of anyone else nearby. Then a figure approached from the dark. "Don't just stand there," he said, his voice slow, as if he was not used to speaking.

"We're not sure what to do?" said Nari. "We were just told to come down here."

The man dropped two buckets down by the truck.

"Empty these into the truck. Then all of those." He indicated the other dozen metal buckets zigzagging their way across the floor of the mine. "When the truck is full you take it to the top. Unload it and then bring it back down. And no more talking. It saps your energy." He walked back towards the sounds of the picks, merging with the dark.

Seo looked at Nari and she shrugged. Seo picked up a bucket, surprised at how heavy it was, steadied it on the side of the truck and tipped it up. The coal rushed out, raising a cloud of dust into the air, and she turned her face away, coughing, holding up her hand in an attempt to filter the air, tasting the coal in her mouth. Min and Nari both took buckets and they began to fill the truck. No matter how many buckets they emptied, there always seemed to be more, brought by silent figures moving back and forth from the hidden coalface, depositing them faster than they could empty them.

They stopped when the truck was full, coal sliding off the top of the heap to the floor. "We better get it to the top," said Min, his voice dry and cracked.

The three of them stood behind the truck and pushed. The wheels seemed well greased and it rolled along fairly easily at first; then they rounded the corner onto the slope. The truck slowed immediately.

"Use the sleepers in the tracks," said Min. "Get a foothold on them."

Seo dug her feet in, using the wooden sleepers to push herself forward, her muscles burning with the effort.

"Keep at it!" said Min. But his voice started to fail, the words coming in gasps. "All together on three... One, two, *three*."

Seo pushed as hard as she could and the truck slid forward.

"Find a foothold. Now again. One two, *three*."

Soon they found their rhythm, no longer having to speak. Seo slipped slowly into a world where there was only the truck and the corrosive pain in her legs and arms. She desperately wanted to stop, to fall onto the floor and try and breathe. But they could only move forward; if they stopped the truck would roll back, crushing them. She barely noticed the other group passing them on their way back down to refill. Almost imperceptivity, the effort became easier as the slope levelled out. Seo felt the light on her face, and with a final heave they burst out of the tunnel into the sunlight.

Seo and Nari collapsed onto the ground, straining for breath. Seo couldn't remember when she had done anything so hard, even half as hard.

"I can't do it again." Nari grabbed Seo by the arm, her eyes wide with shock. "I can't."

"I don't think I can either…"

"Get up!" Seo saw Park striding towards them. "That truck needs to be emptied. Now! And if I catch you resting on the job again it will cost you your rations."

Seo heaved herself onto shaking legs. She grabbed Nari's arm and pulled her up. Min had already begun pushing the truck to the end, and they staggered over and fell against it, shoving it the last few metres to the buffers and the ridge. Below the ridge, a lorry waited on a metal platform, a small pile of coal sitting in the centre of the flatbed.

The coarse handle of the shovel quickly began to rub Seo's hands raw. The coal slipped and fell, and all the time Park shouted, especially if they spilt any. When the truck finally stood empty Park leaned over the side, inspecting every corner. "I want the second one up here and empty in half the time."

Seo glanced down at the lorry. Their truckload of coal didn't seem to have made the slightest difference to the pile. If Park wanted it full, they would all go hungry.

Getting the truck back down felt like a rest. They stood in a line in front of it, their backs taking the weight, and walked slowly down, using the sleepers again to keep steady. At one point Min lost his footing and the truck lurched forward, but they managed to steady it, and continued down to the bottom, where the buckets waited.

They took two more trucks to the surface, and each time Seo didn't think she would make it, bracing herself for the slip that would crush her. She kept singing the song Madam Lim had taught her, repeating it over and over in her head, trying to draw strength from the lyrics, reminding herself of the small slice of forgiveness she earned with each trip. Sometimes she longed to talk to Min and Nari, to see how they felt, what went through their minds. But the prisoner with the buckets had been right: talking sapped energy and they didn't have any to spare.

They had begun loading the fourth truck when the lights went out. There was no warning, no sound, just a sudden immersion in darkness. Seo took a step back and half turned, immediately disorientated. Which way had she been facing?

"Min, Nari. I can't see anything. Where are you."

"I'm here," said Nari. "But I can't see a thing."

"Just stand still," said Min. "You'll trip. The power must have gone. It will come back on soon."

Seo stayed still, expecting her eyes to become accustomed

to the dark, to be able to make out her hands at least; but she could see nothing, only drowning blackness.

"Look out!" The shout tore down the shaft followed by rumbling and the screech of metal on metal.

Seo heard Min's voice. "The other truck. They've let it go! Get off the track. Get off now!"

Had she been standing on the track? Seo wasn't sure. She felt the adrenaline rise with the noise of the freewheeling truck, turning to terror as the sound filled the shaft. Her foot knocked against one of the tracks; she searched with her foot, but couldn't feel the sleepers. *I must be on the side.* She reached out again, stumbled and fell. Her face struck metal and she scrambled to get up, her arms and legs flailing in the darkness. "I don't know which way to go!" She screamed out the words as something rushed past her, the wind almost knocking her back to the floor. A sound like an explosion filled the shaft and she felt dust fly into her eyes. The echoes of the crash drifted slowly away, followed by a shout and then a scream.

"Seo! Seo, where are you?" Nari's voice managed to calm her.

"I'm here. Min...?"

"I'm fine."

The screaming grew quieter and then suddenly stopped.

"Don't move," said Min. "Let's wait until the lights come back on."

Seo stood in the darkness, afraid to move but feeling like she would fall if she didn't get a hand on something to steady her. "Who was screaming?"

"I don't know," said Min. "Just wait."

The lights flickered once, then held. Seo dropped to

her knees, taking deep breaths, ignoring the dust, trying to steady herself. As the dizziness passed she stood and looked back towards the end of the tracks.

The cart lay on its side, twisted and smashed. One of the wheels had flown off and lay against the side of the tunnel. The man who had been carrying the buckets lay on the floor, his legs obscured by the wreckage.

Min walked over to him and knelt down. "He's passed out." Seo walked over and crouched down next to Min. Nari stood back, her hand over her mouth. The man's right leg had jammed between the remains of the cart and the end of the rails, one of the wheels pinning his shin, forcing his foot out at an impossible angle.

"What's going on?" Park strode towards them, followed by the three workers who had let the cart go.

One of the prisoners from the second cart raised his hand. "These three new ones let their cart slip."

"What…?" Seo took a step towards them. "That's not true. You let it go! We were already down here."

"They show no respect for the leaders with their lies."

"Then how come you were up there and not down here?"

The man turned towards Park. "We ran back up straightaway to draw your attention to their negligence."

Seo couldn't believe what she was hearing. It was unnerving to be lied to so forcefully, so confidently.

"Nice try," said Park. "But I saw them go down. You'll lose your rations for this damage. Now get that worker out from under that cart." He took a step forward. "And why can't I hear any digging!" Almost immediately the sound of picks began their disjointed rhythm. The three prisoners from the other cart didn't hesitate, walking quickly towards the wreckage. Seo and Min tried to move the wheel, and the man who had lied so brazenly went over to help. He acted as if nothing had been said, heaving alongside them, even reaching out to steady Seo when she nearly slipped. Seo tried to make sense of his behaviour, but she couldn't.

Once they had cleared the debris, the six of them picked the still-unconscious man up and carried him up the shaft. Outside Seo could see the bloodstains on his trouser leg and a shard of bone sticking through the material. Even under the layer of coal dust he looked pale, his face the colour of an old sheet.

"Well, don't just stand there; we need four more carts in the next hour or we don't make the quota. Move."

They all filed back down the tunnel to the waiting buckets, and when they came up with the next cart, the man had gone, leaving only the lightest indentation of his body in the dust.

NINE

The rat inched towards the scrap of corn, stopping occasionally, its whiskers twitching as it sniffed the ground. Seo lay perfectly still, barely daring to breathe. They hadn't managed to catch anything for days and she willed the rat towards Min's trap with all the concentration she could muster.

Park had shown them how to dry rat meat, as he'd shown them so many things. He had arrived at their hut on the second night, the day they had portioned the building off into separate cells, rubbing at what was left of his hair, sending a cloud of coal dust into the air. At first Seo didn't know how to react – he had been less than friendly in the mine – and she glanced at Nari, seeing the same anxiety on her face as she was feeling herself. Had he come to punish them for something?

"Luxury," said Park, looking around. "Like having your own hotel room." He dropped a small canvas bag onto the floor and squatted down. "There's still twenty of us in one room, and I'm a bloody supervisor. But they might do ours too, I'm told. Apparently smaller groups are easier to control and more suspicious of each other. Or something like that."

Seo looked at Nari, who raised her eyebrows and shrugged.

"Odd they kept you all together, though..." Park seemed to consider this for a moment, staring at a spot on the far wall, then he shrugged. "Never mind, you are together and that's what matters." He slapped his hands together and sat back on his heels. "Right. There is a lot you need to know, but two things are the most important: first, you can trust me. I remember you from town and I enjoyed you coming over to watch the TV; it was nice to have company. But I can't be your friend in the mine, and you mustn't try and be mine. Do you understand?"

The three friends nodded.

"Good. Second, everyone else in the camp is your enemy. People here have only one motivation: to get more food. And they'll do it any way they can. Nothing else matters in here but food. Understand?"

Watching the rat inch towards the trap, Seo understood it better than ever. The rat hesitated, turning its face towards the sky for a moment. Seo looked at Min, lying on the other side of the clearing, her eyes asking if they should rush it, try and catch it with their hands. But he gave a barely perceptible shake of the head, and she tried to relax, to trust the fact the rat was just being cautious, and was just as hungry as she was.

Park had recommended the spot to get water. The river passed close to their hut here, so it meant a short walk. The other prisoners got their water early, so all they had to do was wait for a while and they could usually get the place to themselves. The guard tower had posed a problem, though. Set on a piece of high ground not far from the river, the sentry could see for some distance in all directions, including the clearing. Min had noticed the two prisoners who climbed the tower every day at the same time. From the distance it was difficult to be sure, but they looked like women, and when they had reached the top, the guard disappeared inside, only coming back out when the women had started the climb back down. It gave them thirty minutes when they could be pretty sure no one was watching, but it was still very risky, and Park had warned them of what they could do and what they couldn't.

"Never stray off the paths." Park began to unpack his bag as he spoke, laying the items out in front of him. "The guards are allowed to shoot you on the spot if you do, and some of them will. Understand?"

They nodded.

"If you ever come across a prisoner in a blue uniform, walk the other way; don't even say a word to them. They're the Tainted Bloods, families who have to live in the camp for three generations until their blood is clean again."

"What did they do wrong?" asked Seo.

"Them, nothing. It's what their fathers or grandfathers did and they have to atone for their sins. They don't see the world like us and have no morals whatsoever. Stay away. Clear?"

They nodded.

"Good." He picked up a small cloth bundle, balancing it on his palm and peeling away the layers like wrapping paper to reveal seven strips of meat.

"Help yourself."

Seo didn't hesitate. It was tough and sour, but she chewed on it greedily.

"This has been dried," said Park. "If you try and cook it the guards might smell it, then you're in big trouble."

"Where did you get it?" asked Min, mumbling as he chewed the meat.

"I woke up the other day and it was sitting right next to me."

"What was?"

"The rat."

Seo gagged, but before she could spit it out Park held his hand over her mouth. "Swallow it," he said.

Somehow Seo managed to swallow the piece of rat meat and sat, gasping for a moment, trying not to throw up.

"It's not that bad," said Min. He had bitten his in half and looked at the remaining piece with a scientific curiosity before popping it into his mouth.

Nari looked at Park in horror. "I just ate rat…? Are you kidding…?"

"You need the protein. The mush they feed us on here is mostly corn and you'll end up with pellagra if you don't get meat."

"What is that?" asked Seo.

"Disease caused by protein deficiency. It starts off as just a rash but gets very nasty if your diet doesn't change."

"How nasty?" Min sounded more interested than worried.

"Madness then death. Besides, there are plenty of worse things to eat," said Park, tossing another piece of rat meat into his mouth. "Before too long this will taste as good as barbecued pork."

Lying on the ground, the dusk gathering, their dinner still

hesitating in front of the trap, Seo involuntarily licked her lips. She had never had barbecued pork, but she didn't gag when she ate rat anymore – it was the best thing they had to eat. She felt a tap on her ankle and looked across at Nari, who arched her eyebrows towards the watchtower. Seo looked up, trying to guess the time, but she knew if they hadn't caught it in the next few minutes they would have to give up.

She got ready to stand, to make the walk back to the hut with nothing, when the rat darted forward, snatching up the corn in its mouth. Min yanked at the cord and the small wooden cage dropped. The rat squealed, the trap shaking and jarring as the rat tried to shake it off. The three off them set off at the same time, but Nari reached it first, diving for the trap, pressing her hands down just as the rat's head appeared under the edge. It squealed again, dragging its face back under the bars. Nari held the trap tight, looking at Min, who nodded, and she lifted the edge slightly just as Min thrust his hand underneath, dragging the rat out and hitting it twice against the ground. The rat went limp.

"Heads up," said Seo. The two women had begun their descent down from the tower.

Min stuffed the rat down the front of his trousers and the three of them set off as casually as they could, just as the guard emerged onto the platform of his tower. They still had plenty of time before the final siren, so Seo didn't worry or try and hurry, but even at that pace Min started dropping behind. They passed other prisoners and a guard, who gave them a quick glance before turning away. Seo slowed, allowing Min to catch up, and Nari did the same, until they walked side by side.

"What's the matter?" whispered Seo.

Min swallowed hard, his shoulders giving a sudden twitch. "The rat's not dead."

"Are you sure?"

"Pretty sure!"

"Is it going to escape?"

"I've got it by the tail through the hole in my pocket. It's pretty groggy, but definitely waking up." Both his legs jerked and he stumbled forward.

"Nearly there," said Seo. "Hang on."

"Stop there!"

The three froze on the spot, Seo trying to keep her eyes on the ground but not able to resist looking up to see who had shouted. Hwan, the guard who had taken them to the mine, strode towards them, his uniform as immaculate as ever, the shine on his shoes catching the sun. He stopped in front of them and leaned forward, Seo catching the stink of his breath, as if underneath all the creases and starch something rotted deep inside him.

"What's wrong with you?" shouted Hwan, jabbing a finger towards Min's face. "You're walking all over the place."

Seo had seen guards stop and search prisoners many times, and if Hwan decided to do that, they would lose their rat and maybe even their visits to the clearing. "He's sick, sir," she said, bowing as low as she could, the thought and words forming simultaneously.

"Sick?" said Hwan.

"Stomach trouble. Vomiting and terrible diarrhoea. It gets all over his trousers and makes him walk funny."

Hwan took a step back, and Min pushed the advantage, bringing his hand to his mouth. "I think I'm going to puke again."

"Get out of here!" shouted Hwan. "And if he's not fit to work tomorrow, none of you get any rations."

"Yes, sir. Thank you, sir."

They hurried away, Seo putting a hand on Min's shoulder. They rounded the corner of their building and fell through the door, Nari backing up against it. Min pulled the rat from his trousers, its legs running in mid-air, bashed it against the wall and hid it under his sheet. They waited in silence for a moment, making sure Hwan had been repulsed enough not to follow, then Seo let herself sink to the ground. "That was close."

Nari snorted, lifting her hand to her face to hide her smile. Seo suddenly found she had to do the same, putting a finger into her mouth and biting down, trying to stave off the laughter with pain, finally giving in, letting it run free.

"You think it's funny?" said Min, trying to hide his own smile. "Next time it's going down one of your trousers."

TEN

eo met Iseul on the day the first snow fell. She pushed the cart up the mineshaft with Nari and Min, gasping in the fresh air as they came out to grey skies.

Min flicked his head towards the path. "More guards are coming," he whispered.

"What does that mean?" Nari stared at the approaching figures. "Oh no. I think one of them is Hwan."

"Great," said Seo. "Compassionate Comrade of the Year is early today."

Hwan and the other guard strode towards them. They stopped and talked briefly to the sentries, before Hwan turned and made his way down the hill, leaving the other guard walking towards them. Seo breathed out in relief. If Hwan wasn't there, whatever the other one wanted couldn't be too bad.

"You!" He pointed at Seo. "Come with me."

Seo bowed her head and took a step forward. "Yes, sir."

She glanced back at the others, seeing the concern in their eyes, but she knew better than to ask what the guard wanted, so she kept her head down and followed him away from the mine. They walked past the meal hut and down a slope towards the centre of the camp. The guard said nothing and Seo felt her legs beginning to weaken, trying to think of a reason as to why the guard wanted her.

They stopped on the path overlooking the logging factory, the smell of sawdust drifting up to her on an icy breeze. A body lay on the path next to a small wooden cart. It was a boy, not much older than Seo, one leg caught under his body, his face staring out towards the mountains.

"Take the body to the graveyard before it starts to stink the place up. Follow the path straight on, then get back to the mine. No resting." The guard spoke as if he was telling Seo to fetch water or dig a hole, his voice showing no emotion, and he walked down towards the logging factory without another word.

Seo stared at the body, not quite believing what she had to do. She glanced in the direction the guard had gone, but he walked quickly and didn't look back. She walked around to the boy's head and squeezed her shaking hands under his shoulders. She heaved him up and dragged him towards the cart, twisting her body to try and get him on. He bumped against the side, the cart toppling over, and the body hit the ground with a thump. Seo righted the cart and tried again, but she couldn't lift the body high enough and it kept hitting the side, knocking it over. Each time she had to pick it up again she felt her nerves tighten under the strain, a deep sense of anxiety building in her stomach. She moved the cart a little way down the path and set it against a large rock. She dragged the boy over and, with the rock holding the cart upright, managed to heave his shoulders on, pulling the top half of his body across the wood. She bent down and lifted his legs, swinging them up. The boy lay on the cart, his head hanging between the handles, mouth open, his arms and legs dangling over the sides. She took the handles, trying to avoid looking at the boy's face, wishing she could close his eyes, and set off down the track.

The rutted path meant Seo struggled to keep the cart from falling. Twice the wheel stuck and it took all her strength to get it moving again. She tried not to look at the boy, keeping her eyes in the distance, trying to tell herself that it was just a corpse, she had seen them before, and it was nothing to be afraid of. But a voice kept whispering in her ear: *you've never been this close to death before, you've never been this close...*

A dog barked and she dropped the handles in shock, fighting back tears, stunned that such a simple sound could cause such fear. The path had taken her towards the perimeter fence and two guards walked past, one holding the leash of an Alsatian that strained forwards, its front legs rising off the ground. He said something to his companion, who laughed, and they walked on.

Seo had never been so close to the fence before. A low hum vibrated in the air, and she realised the fence was electrified. A stretch of sand, about two metres wide, ran along its base, raked smooth, snaking into the distance. She could see three watchtowers set at the edge of the sand, their whitewash streaked and greying. The guard in the one nearest to her let the barrel of his rifle fall into his palm, turning his body towards her. She quickly put her head down, picked up the cart and pushed on.

The path led her away from the fence and the boring eyes of the watchtowers, and she relaxed a little, the concentration needed to keep the cart level helping her to forget what lay across its boards.

"Hello."

The voice made her jump as much as the dog had, but this time she couldn't control the cart and the body slipped off onto the ground.

Seo looked up to see a boy squatting on a flat rock just above her head, his arms resting on his knees. His uniform looked different from the other prisoners and Seo thought it must have been blue once.

"What are you doing up there?" said Seo. "Look at what you made me do!"

Seo took a step back as the boy jumped down onto the path, landing lightly next to the cart, his hands resting on the ground for a moment before he jumped to his feet. Shorter than Seo, he had close-cropped hair that looked like it had been cut with a knife. Half his left ear was missing and he had lines on his face that almost looked like wrinkles, but his eyes looked young, and as he scratched his cheek Seo saw his hands showed no signs of age. It was impossible to guess how old he was.

"I don't see-snitch you marching here before," he said.

"What?"

The boy tutted. "You don't march here before." He walked on the spot for a moment, each word slow and carefully enunciated, as if Seo spoke a foreign language or was some kind of idiot.

"I know what you mean. I'm not stupid. You speak funny, that's all."

The boy considered this for a moment, then shrugged. "The man in the cages think this. He spoke like crushers too."

"Crushers?"

He pointed an imaginary rifle at Seo and pulled the trigger.

"Oh, guards. Yes, I suppose I do. I thought everybody did. Why don't you?"

The boy shrugged, staring at the body on the ground, as if something didn't quite make sense to him. "Your shift is to march to the dead-holes?"

It only took Seo a moment to translate the sentence in her mind. "Yes, I have to take this body there."

The boy took a step forward, a smile on his face, and he clapped his hands. "My name is Iseul."

"I'm Seo," she said. Everything about Iseul confused her: the way he talked, his clothes, his reactions. She couldn't understand why anyone would look so happy at the news she had to take a corpse to the graves.

"Next shift you are marching this way? The next one, the next one?"

"I hope not. I work in the mine and I need to get back there. I don't want to do this again."

Iseul ignored her, looking at the body on the ground and then at Seo, his eyes widening as if he had just solved a riddle. "Why you don't sneak-carry the clothes?"

"What?"

"Why you don't sneak-carry?" He gestured to the corpse with both hands, as if not quite believing that Seo could have forgotten to do something so important. "The boots look warmly." He moved towards the body, his hands reaching out.

"Stop it," said Seo. "Leave him alone." She stepped forward, putting herself between Iseul and the dead boy, the thought of stripping a corpse for its clothes sending a wave of repulsion through her. "You mustn't take anything!"

Iseul shrugged, tapping his finger against the side of his head, looking at her in bewilderment. "He's your dead-dead. But others will sneak-carry at the dead-holes—"

"That's none of my business. They can do what they want." She glanced down the path, suddenly worried she had been talking too long. "I'm going to be in trouble if I don't get going. A guard will come along soon and we shouldn't be talking."

Iseul smiled, wagging his finger at her. "No crushers on this stretch. Only start-shift and end-shift when everyone is marching. That's why I rest here. Only one other place like this in the world."

"The world?" Seo had already begun to lift the body back onto the cart, but it kept slipping. "Can you help me?"

Iseul looked away before squatting down on the path and folding his arms.

"Please," said Seo. "It's too hard on my own."

"Will you snitch to me about the outside?"

"What?"

Iseul made a sweeping gesture with his arm. "Outside the world."

Seo stopped trying to heave the body and looked at him. "You've never been outside the camp?"

He shook his head. "I can't carry or march with you. But I once met a man in the cages for sneak-carrying corn from the ground. He marched from the outside too and he snitched to me about cars and houses and having warmly mush with rice and meat every shift. Is it real?"

He was a Tainted Blood, born in the camps, sentenced for the crimes of his parents or grandparents, and as the knowledge settled in her mind, she felt a growing anxiety. Park had warned them never to trust them, not even speak to them, but something about him fascinated her. "Sometimes."

Iseul clapped his hands. "I help you move the dead-dead, you snitch to me about outside. Warmly trade!" He turned around, giving Seo his full attention, like a child waiting for a story. "Did you have meat every shift?"

"In Pyongyang I did."

"Where's Pyongyang?"

"No more talking until I've got this body back on the cart."

Iseul stood and, steadying the cart with his leg, pulled the body up with ease. "How do I march to Pyongyang?"

Seo let out a laugh. "They won't let you go to Pyongyang."

"Why? You marched."

"That was different. I had to do something important. Not everyone can go there, only people chosen by the leaders."

"Like the Great Commuter?"

"The Great *Commander*," said Seo. "They must have taught you about him in school."

"They taught me how to sew clothes and chop trees. The man in the cage snitched to me about the commander."

Seo knew talking could get her beaten if she was caught, but she couldn't draw herself away, suddenly wanting to know how someone could go through life not knowing all the things she did. If he was right and no guards came along this stretch then she had a few minutes…

"The Great Commander is the father of our nation. He loves us and we are his children. He is the sun that shines on our lives."

Iseul looked up at the sky. "Here is the sun," he said.

Seo laughed again. "It's not literal."

"I can't understand."

"It means that his love is so strong for us, it's like the love the sun gives the flowers."

Iseul thought about this for a second. "I don't think he shines on me very warmly."

"Look, don't think about him as a sun, think about him as a father."

"He will beat me?"

"You shouldn't say things like that!" said Seo.

Iseul shrugged. "All right. I can't make sense anyway. Sounds upside down."

"I better go," said Seo.

"Wait. You haven't told me the marching to Pyongyang."

"You can't even get out of the camp. You're not going to get to Pyongyang."

"Maybe not so hard. But I don't know which way to march afterwards."

The words hit Seo like a punch in the stomach. It was a trick. He would try and get her to say she wanted to leave the camp and then snitch. It would be worth a lot of food to stop a prisoner from escaping.

"I'm reporting you!" she said, grabbing the cart and pushing it down the track. "You shouldn't say such things."

"Don't carry yet," said Iseul. "I won't snitch to the crushers. I just want to hear about the mush."

But Seo didn't stop, desperate to get away. The cart hit

a hole and the body slid to one side, she grabbed at it, just managing to stop it from falling. She glanced back, but Iseul had vanished.

The sound of a guard shouting told her she must be close to the graveyard, and she tried to push the cart a little faster. The path widened, and she caught sight of the river and a corn farm out in the distance, before finding herself on a large plateau. About a dozen prisoners worked with shovels, some digging, others scooping earth back into graves. A guard stood in each corner, rifles slung over their shoulders. Seo looked around, expecting to see Iseul whispering in a guard's ear, telling him she wanted to escape. But the guards paid her no attention and she relaxed a little. She looked around the graveyard, unsure of what to do, until a prisoner looked up and pointed towards a freshly dug grave. The soft ground made pushing the cart even harder than it had been on the path, but she made it without the body falling.

"Stop!" A prisoner walked over to her, his armband marking him out as a supervisor. "You haven't been here before, have you?" he asked.

Seo shook her head.

"You can't bury him like that. Too much waste." He pulled the boy's boots off and looked at them, grunting in satisfaction, before stripping the corpse naked. It took him no more than a minute. The boy had wrapped some material around his chest, a makeshift vest, and the supervisor rubbed the fabric between his thumb and fingers, then looked at Seo. "Here," he said, throwing it to her. "It's warm."

Seo caught it, the feel of the material outweighing her disgust. "Thank you."

The man tipped the cart up, spilling the body into the

hole. It lay face down, one arm under its body, the other reaching out to the side of the grave.

"You can go," said the man.

Seo turned, hurrying back the way she had come, desperate to be with Min and Nari again, to feel the warmth of their company, let it wipe away the image of the naked boy that had been printed on her mind, as a flurry of snowflakes swept down from the sky.

ELEVEN

The three friends sat by the opening to the mine, their shoulders slumped. Nari wiped at her face, trying to clear away the dust, but she just smeared it around. The workers from the pit-face sat nearby next to the other team of cart pushers. Seo coughed, spitting out black phlegm. Nobody spoke and there were no other sounds, no birdsong or machinery noise, as if the camp itself had shut down in exhaustion.

Seo hadn't told the others about Iseul, or the boy she had wheeled to the cemetery to be stripped and dumped in an unmarked grave. She told them she had to carry some wood for the guards and knew they hadn't believed her, but they didn't pursue it. She thought about Iseul often, saw his face light up with joy at the idea of rice and meat in the same meal, and the more she saw it the more uncomfortable the image became, but she couldn't work out why.

She looked up at the sound of footsteps and saw Hwan

walking towards them, flanked, as always, by two other guards carrying rifles. Park ran over to them holding his clipboard and they all walked to the truck, where their day's quota of coal lay waiting. The anticipation of the result banished Iseul from her mind. Sometimes they had made it, sometimes they hadn't, but she was pretty sure they had that day; she could feel it in her legs.

"Do you think about your parents much?"

Nari's question took Seo by surprise and she opened her eyes, sitting up a little to look at her friend. "Of course. All the time. Mostly at night, though, before I go to sleep. They must worry about us." She picked up a small stone on the ground and tossed it a few feet in front of her. "You?"

Nari nodded. "Every day. All the time." She turned her face away and Seo put her hand on her shoulder.

"It's all right. We'll see them again soon."

"I worry about my mum," said Min. "She's not very... practical. If something broke, there's no one there to fix it for her."

"I'm sure the others in her block will help."

"I'm not sure. I'm afraid they will see her as Hostile Class now, because of what I did." Min swallowed hard, fiddling with a stray thread from his trousers. "I worry they might have sent her to a camp as well."

"Don't say that!"

Min jerked back, the shock at the anger in Nari's voice lingering in his eyes. "I'm sorry, Nari. I didn't mean anything—"

"Hey!" Seo put her hand on Nari's shoulder. "It's all right. They send whole families off together." She stretched out her other hand to Min. "If they were in a camp, they'd be in this one." She squeezed Nari's arm, then turned and looked at Min. "Right?"

"We're all clear! Let's eat!" Park's voice stopped any further conversation as they scrambled to their feet and began the trek around the side of the mine to the long wooden shack.

As always, a soldier stood by the table at the far end stirring the huge pot, the prisoners jostling for a position in the queue. One by one the soldier filled each bowl with a ladleful from the pot, everyone hurrying back to their seats, holding their bowls close, as if afraid someone might snatch it away from them. Seo took her bowl, feeling the warmth run through her hands, loving the sight of a small amount of corn boiled to a mush with a few soya beans sitting on the top. She rushed back to her seat and devoured it, licking every drop from the bottom and sides of the bowl, cleaning it in moments. She looked up to see Min and Nari staring at their now-empty bowls. It was never enough – not nearly enough. Seo remembered the meals she had had in Pyongyang: rice and meat three times a day, but she tried to block the smells and tastes from her mind, the memories doubling her pain. Around her the other prisoners ate slowly, some pausing between mouthfuls, savouring every scrap.

"Stand!" Park barked out the order and Seo nearly fell as the bench was pushed out from under her. Hwan strode through the door and stood at the far end of the hut.

Great, thought Seo. Ideological Struggle.

She helped the other prisoners carry the tables to the end of the hut and arrange the benches in a rough circle so they all sat facing each other across the room. When everyone had sat, Hwan circled behind them, stopping occasionally behind a prisoner, something that always sent a shiver through Seo's body. He made a complete circuit before speaking, Seo miming the words in her head, like she used to in Mr Chi's lessons whenever he recited something she had learnt by heart:

"It is time for you to reflect on your crimes and your failures today in making amends for them. Ideological Struggle is as important to your rehabilitation as the manual work you perform."

Seo glanced up at Nari, bringing a hand up to hide her smile as she saw her lips murmuring along with Hwan.

He pointed to one of the prisoners who had had their food denied to them. "Why did you receive no rations today?"

The man stood, his head bowed, cloth-cap in his hand, and explained how he had fallen behind due to an injury to his leg.

"You show no respect!" shouted Hwan. "You fail to meet your work quota after our leaders have given you this chance! Shown their love for you!" He punched the man on the side of the head, knocking him to the ground. "Then you dare to give excuses?"

Ideological Struggle didn't happen every day, but Seo couldn't determine a pattern. It seemed to be whenever Hwan wanted, and this was the first session in several days. She had attended self-criticism since she could remember but had never experienced anything as violent as this.

The man picked himself up from the ground, standing unsteadily. "I have failed the leaders but will never allow such a thing to happen again."

"Sit," said Hwan, turning to another prisoner, but before he could speak, the door opened and Colonel Nam walked in, his white hair shining under the light. He stared at the scene for a moment, only his eyes moving as he surveyed the room, then signalled to Hwan. The two spoke for a moment, then Nam took a seat in the corner of the room and lit a cigarette.

Hwan approached the prisoner he had been about to address and then turned suddenly to face Min. "You!"

Min stood immediately, his hands behind his back.

"List your failings today."

They had all become imaginative story-tellers with a repertoire of failings they could draw on when needed.

"I stopped for a moment when pushing the cart. It was selfish and showed no respect."

Hwan nodded slowly, as if weighing up this piece of information. "And how should you be punished for this?"

Min looked at Seo, surprise and worry on his face. Hwan had never asked that question before, and Seo felt as lost as Min looked.

"I… I…"

"Speak up!"

Min looked at Seo again and opened his mouth to speak just as Nam punched him on the jaw, sending him sliding across the floor, his glasses clattering against the wall as he hit one of the benches. He lay, clutching his jaw and gasping for breath. Seo put her hand to her mouth, stifling a cry. Across the room a tear slid down Nari's face, leaving a trail through the coal dust.

Hwan turned to Nari, walking slowly around her chair and stopping behind her. He took a bamboo cane that rested against the wall and slowly ran it down Nari's arm then her leg, drawing it slowly back up to come to a rest on her shoulder. He began tapping the cane against her, the wood hitting cloth creating a muffled beat.

"And what did you do wrong today?"

Nari began to tremble, her eyes locked on Seo, pleading and terrified.

Hwan started tapping the cane harder, raising it a little higher each time. Nari flinched with each stroke, slowly lowering her shoulder, trying to ease the growing pain.

Hwan put on a face of feigned puzzlement. "I wonder how long I could keep this up?"

Anger exploded in Seo, and before she knew what she was doing, she was on her feet, her fist clenched.

Hwan strode towards her, a slight smile on his face. "You've got something to say, little sparrow?"

Seo faltered, Hwan's voice taking away some of the anger. Min stared up at her from his position on the floor, slowly but deliberately shaking his head.

The urge to spit in Hwan's face grew unbearable, and it took every ounce of self-control for Seo to back down. "I wished to share that I have also failed today." She forced the words out, each syllable an effort.

Hwan glanced at Nam then pushed Seo back into her seat. "You'll get your turn."

Seo looked over at Nam. He stared at her, a cigarette dangling from his lips, a look of intense disappointment on his face, then stood and strode out of the door.

Hwan seemed to take this as a cue and ordered the prisoners to stand. They recited the laws of the camp and headed out, walking in silence back to the huts, the guards that flanked them just shadows in a moonless night.

Interview 6

Days Since Arrest:	15
Time:	10:30
Location:	Interview Room 4
Subject:	Jane Doe
Age:	Unknown
Origin:	Unknown
Medical Condition:	Evidence of severe physical trauma
	Evidence of Post-Traumatic Stress Disorder
	Inability to speak

Interviewing Officer: Kim Soo Jung

X – *Good morning. How are you today?*

NO RESPONSE.

X – *Do you remember last time we met, you wrote something down for me? Do you remember that?*

NO RESPONSE.

X – I've brought some paper and a pen. I was hoping you would write some other things down for me. Would you do that?

SUBJECT TAKES THE PAPER AND PENCIL.

X – *OK! That's great. You can take all the time you need. You can even take it back to your room. It might be easier if you pretend you're writing about someone else. Do you think you can do that?*

SUBJECT BEGINS TO WRITE.

X – *Thank you. I often find if I write something down it helps me see things a lot clearer.*

Interview Terminated: 10:43

TWELVE

She had never really doubted her faith in the leaders or the Party; it had been as solid as the ground she walked on, only made clearer by her time in Pyongyang. But since she had wheeled the boy's body to the graves and Hwan had beaten Min and Nari, she had felt a shift inside her, one that she couldn't explain but sensed was important. The world she knew carried on as usual: days in the mine gasping for breath, Hwan punching and slapping his way through Ideological Struggle, making them stand and point at their colleagues, lie about their friends or people they barely knew. Thankfully, Nam had not returned, and Seo and the others hadn't been subject to any more special attention, and she drifted through the days, numb, her mind distant from the mine, the canteen, Hwan and his flailing arms; her eyes always fixed on the boy lying in his grave and her ears hearing only Iseul's voice: ...*I can't make sense anyway.*

Her feet crunched through the snow as they walked back to their hut. Min and Nari kept looking at her, and she knew they wanted to talk, to find out what was wrong, but she didn't know what to say. Her heart had filled with words and sounds, but ones she couldn't quite make out, whispers floating just out of reach.

"Come on," said Min. "Let's get this fire going."

Min's voice broke Seo out of her trance, and she realised they were back in the hut – Nari brushing snow from her shoulders, Min rekindling the embers of the fire. If they damped it down with ash before they left, they often didn't need to light it again.

"It's getting so cold," said Nari. "I never thought I'd be glad to work in a mine, but at least you're out of the wind." She coughed, and Seo could hear the phlegm rattling in her chest.

Seo sat down next to her.

"So, you going to tell us what's wrong?"

"Nothing," said Seo. "I'm just…"

"Tired?"

"Probably." Seo looked at her friend. Some of the light seemed to have faded from her eyes; her lips had lost the colour that all the girls had envied her for; her hair hung matted around her cheeks, as full of lice as Seo's.

Min got out the small metal saucepan that Park had brought on one of his visits and filled it with some moss and grasses they had been saving. He poured over a little water and set it by the fire. "We'll need to get more water tomorrow. And it's going to be much harder to find food now the snow has come."

Min had lost the most weight. His cheeks had begun to

sink into his face and his hand trembled as he stirred the pot. The cracked lens in his glasses had shattered a few days earlier when a slap from Hwan had sent them flying across the room again. Seo wondered how much more weight he could afford to lose.

The image of the boy she had buried still wouldn't leave her. It hovered in the corner of her eye, following her wherever she went, whatever she did. What had he done, she thought, to be thrown in here, left dead on the side of a path for a stranger to strip and throw in a pit? She touched the vest the supervisor had given her. He had been right, it was warm, but it hadn't saved its owner. She thought of Iseul, born in a camp that he would never be allowed to leave. For what? Something his grandfather had done? She closed her eyes, trying to bring the song she should have sung at the festival to her heart, to recall the love she had felt for the leaders and her country, to sing away the doubts. But it wouldn't come. Instead she heard the song from the radio and saw her father sitting in the cart on their way home from the executions.

… that's what they tell us, isn't it?

A draught hit the fire, sending ash and smoke into her eyes. She coughed and wiped away the tears.

Nari prodded the pan with a stick. "Will it be ready soon?"

"It's only just gone on," said Min. "It'll take a while to soften."

Seo slowly wrote a single word in the dust by her side, drawing the characters with care: *Why?* She stared at it for a moment, retracing the lines with her finger.

"Why did they put us in here?" Seo didn't ask the question

to anyone in particular, just allowing the words to form from the snowstorm of thoughts in her head.

For a moment nobody spoke, Min staring at Seo as if he was afraid of the question.

"They put us in here because we listened to a radio," said Seo. "That's right, isn't it?" She stopped, reassuring herself it was correct. "We listened to a radio."

"You shouldn't talk about that," said Min. "We're here to forget all about it, to put it behind us."

"We found a radio buried in the ground, switched it on and it played stuff from the South."

"Stop it, Seo," hissed Nari, pointing to the wall. "People are probably listening."

"And wasn't it amazing stuff? How can it be so wrong to have listened to it? Remember those stories that they tell in the South? Not about leaders or heroes, but ordinary people who can do wonderful things—"

"Seo!"

"…and songs. So many songs, but that first one we heard will always be my favourite; it just won't go away. I've tried to forget it, I really have, but I can't. It was beauty. Nothing more, nothing less – just beauty. I can still remember the tune now."

"Don't, Seo," said Nari, her voice pleading. "They'll hear."

Seo started to sing the song, not trying to pronounce the alien lyrics, just letting the tune take its course. She didn't want a beating from the guards any more than anyone else, but she couldn't help herself. Something inside her told her that if she didn't sing then, she never would; that part of her would die, buried with the boy in the snow. The song they had heard the day they found the radio had become the hill outside the town where they foraged for food, the taste of her mother's cooking and the warmth in her father's eyes. Laughter and love danced with the melody, and she needed to feel those things again.

The last note stayed in the air long after Seo finished. Min looked at her, frozen, holding his stirring-stick in mid-air, the stew of grass and bark forgotten.

Seo stared at the door, waiting for it to be thrown open and guards to rush in. But no one came, and at that moment, she wouldn't have cared if they did.

"I think we got away with it," said Nari.

Min snapped out of his trance and began to spoon stew into their plastic bowls, a present from Park on one of his visits. "It was nice to hear you sing, Seo. But we shouldn't take risks like that. The rest of the hut must have heard it."

"None of the rules say 'no singing'," said Seo.

Min laughed. "True, I suppose."

Seo took some soup, tipping the bowl up and drinking it down, feeling the warmth slip from her throat all the way to her stomach. "I loved those stories too. My favourite was *Blossoms on the Moon*."

"Me too," said Nari, some of her reticence falling away. "There were so many people in it: a student, a taxi driver, a doctor, an engineer, a pilot and a few others. I can't remember all of them."

"I wanted to be a pilot," said Min. "Ever since I was very young."

"You never said that before," said Nari.

"I always thought they were the most amazing machines, that the people who built them must be so clever. But to fly one... to be in the sky like a bird."

"I wanted to be a doctor." Nari blushed slightly as she spoke, turning her face away a little, as if she was worried the others would think the idea absurd. "But I know I'm not clever enough."

They fell into silence for a while. There had been no need to ask Seo what she wanted to do, and everyone knew it didn't matter anyway. Min would have been assigned to the canning factory or the rice store and Nari would have sewn blankets or uniforms for the army. Only Seo had been given a chance to follow her dream, and that had gone now, a candle carried away into the dark.

"Do you remember that episode when the doctor found out his girlfriend was married?" said Seo, trying to banish the depression that had started to settle over her mind. "I'll never forget that meal he had cooked. I didn't know you could have so much food in one place."

"I remember that one," said Min. "But my favourite was when the bank robbers made the taxi driver be their getaway car—"

"No one believed he was innocent at first," said Seo, "but they had jumped into his cab when their car broke down and made him drive at gunpoint."

Nari face lit up as the memories came back to her. "They sent him to prison for a while until they found the robbers and he got off."

They told as many stories from the radio as they could remember, sometimes stopping to correct each other, filling in the details that someone else had forgotten. Soon they were acting out the parts, Min dropping his voice to a bass to play the doctor, while Nari simpered and fawned as his cheating girlfriend. Seo put an imaginary gun to the side of Min's head, and he pretended to be the taxi driver, his car screaming down imaginary roads, as he begged in silent screams to let him stop. Nari became a law student, desperately trying to finish her work but tempted by the party she could hear going on in the flat next door. And finally Min took control of his passenger jet, taking off towards Tokyo, the others his passengers, talking about the sights they would see in Japan.

The end came naturally, their memories emptying and tiredness taking over. They spread out their blankets near the fire, each in their own spot, a little space at night they could call their own. The fire had started to drop, just leaves of flame fluttering in the draughts as silence settled into the hut.

"It's a shame it's all just propaganda," said Min, in not much more than a yawn.

"Yes," said Seo. "That's what they tell us, isn't it?"

Neither of them replied, sleep seeming to come quickly and easily to Min and Nari.

Seo lay awake, listening to the breathing of the others. Nari coughed regularly, her body jerking with the strain. Min made no sound, his breathing slow and regular. Seo reached over and pulled her small suitcase towards her, reaching inside and pulling out the badge that her teacher, Mr Chi, had given to her in the classroom that day, and she thought about what he had told her, his unwavering loyalty to the Party and its leaders. She stared at the face of the Great Commander, smiling benevolently at her, an orange glow framing his face. She ran her finger across the enamel. "Are you lying to me?" she whispered.

But no answer came, just his eternal smile as the last flames of the fire began to flicker and the wind slapped against the walls of the hut.

THIRTEEN

They stopped in an open space flanked on three sides by whitewashed walls. A wooden platform sat at the far end with a pole jutting up from the back topped with another running parallel to the platform. A guard approached and flung a length of rope across the top pole. He fastened one end to the platform, leaving a noose dangling about six feet from the ground. A gust of wind caught it, leaving it swaying back and forth, like a pendulum from a giant clock.

They had lined up outside the hut as usual, but instead of Park marching them away to the mine, they had joined other prisoners and headed in the opposite direction. The path led down to the centre of the camp, past the logging factory and out towards the barren cornfields. The wind began to pick up, whipping snow in her face. They passed a row of buildings that looked like housing blocks; the last one had collapsed, leaving nothing but a sloping pile of rubble, half-covered by snow. In the distance she caught sight of the main entrance, a group of newly arrived prisoners standing in front of the list of camp rules, a guard pointing to each one with a stick. One of them began to cry, dropping her small bundle of clothes. The guard walked up and slapped her across the face. The woman screamed and ran towards the entrance, banging on the door, and Seo could hear the guard ordering her to stop. Realising she wouldn't get back through the door she ran past the gate towards the fence, reaching out with both her hands. A shower of sparks erupted from the fence with a sound like a gunshot. The woman clung to the wire, her body convulsing, flames eating away at her clothes, before falling back into the snow.

"Stop!" ordered one of the guards.

Seo and the others did as they were told, everyone staring at the woman's body, wisps of smoke rising up from where she lay in the snow. Seo wondered who would get her boots. They looked warm and strong.

She couldn't see Min and Nari, the space being only just big enough for all of them, and she had been squashed in the middle, two rows from the front. The morning light had begun to stretch across the horizon but hadn't yet pushed back the dark. No one will notice if I close my eyes, she thought. I won't have to watch. Memories of the stadium in her town came back to her, of the *Immiban*, Mrs Kim, with her megaphone and the prisoners shot to their knees by the soldiers. She expected to feel the same fear and stress but could only wonder how long they would be kept in the cold.

Nam strode onto the platform, his greatcoat buttoned up to his chin, his eyes scanning the group of prisoners in front of him. Seo turned her face away, not wanting to catch his eye, but she felt his gaze come to rest on her as firmly as if he had walked up and touched her.

"Today you will witness one who has refused to accept his crimes." Nam spoke slowly and clearly, the words enunciated in clouds of condensed breath. "This man has been known to be a corrupter of youth, abusing his position as a teacher to fill the minds of his students with the lies of the imperialists. Despite the mercy of the state giving him a chance here to redeem himself he has refused to confess to his crimes. He has become irredeemable and will be hanged until he is dead." He nodded to the guard, who walked behind the wall and returned with a prisoner. His hands had been tied in front of him and a hood pulled down over his head, his uniform stained and bloodied, his left shoulder exposed where the material had torn. The guard turned the man so he faced the crowd and ripped off his hood.

Seo couldn't stifle the cry, her hand reaching her mouth an instant too late. There in front of her on the platform stood her teacher Mr Chi. He looked around, his tiny frame shaking so much it seemed he might fall apart. He lifted his chin and tried to straighten his shoulders, but he kept jerking forward, the cold taking control of his movements.

"Chi Mi Cheung, you have refused to acknowledge your crimes against the motherland and have been sentenced to death," shouted Nam, his face towards the crowd, ignoring the shivering figure of Seo's teacher.

Mr Chi looked around at the buildings and the people in front of him, as if not quite believing what he saw. "What is this place?" he asked, his voice quiet and brittle.

Nam turned to him and opened his mouth to speak, but before he could Mr Chi's eyes met Seo's. His mouth opened in shock. "Oh, not you, my child. Run, Seo Jun! Run! They must be spies, do not believe them, you must—"

But he never finished, his words cut off by a grinding noise then a thump. His body dropped, jerking to a stop, his feet a few inches from the ground.

"No!" screamed Seo, pushing her way through the people in front of her, desperate to get to him, to hold him up, to stop what was happening. "You can't! You mustn't!" She broke free from the crowd, rushing towards the scaffold, desperate to reach him. "He's my teacher. He's a good man, you—" Something hit her back and she tripped, falling towards the scaffold, her arms reaching out. Pain shot through her skull; she saw a flash of light then darkness.

• • •

For a moment Seo couldn't open her eyes; they felt glued together. A headache the size of a rice ball throbbed just above her right ear. She tried to move her hand to feel, but neither arm would budge, trapped somewhere above her head. Her eyes blinked open, catching snapshots of her surroundings, before the world came slowly into focus. They had put her in a cage, about two feet shorter than she was, a criss-cross of rusty metal bands with an opening just in front of her face. Her arms had been tied above her head, keeping her upright while she had been unconscious, the pain from the rope burns building as her senses crept back to her. She tried to stand, but her head hit the top, and if she tried to sit the ropes on her arms kept her up, forcing her to crouch, knees bent. In front of her a brazier burned, too far away to feel the heat but close enough to smell the smoke that curled through the night air.

"So you are awake." Nam's voice came from behind and Seo tried to turn to see him, but the cage walls held her tight.

"Tell me. Was it worth it?"

Seo kept quiet, not sure what to do.

"There he is. Look up, just past the brazier." He sounded like someone pointing out a rare bird or beautiful sunset.

Seo looked, squinting her eyes in the dark. They had left her in the execution square, the scaffold still in place, the body of her teacher hanging by the rope, his head cocked to one side, his toes brushing the snow.

"You tried to save a traitor. A spy. I was worried one of the guards might shoot you on the spot. But I managed to stop them in time."

Seo swallowed, trying to get enough moisture in her mouth to speak. "He fought with the Great Commander. He was loyal."

She heard Nam move behind her, and her body tensed, her aching knees trembling.

"It's true. But why would a man like that choose to stay in a small town when he could have had the glory of Pyongyang? He was a spy, trying to corrupt the youth. Three of his students have already been arrested and the people of your town will be much more vigilant now. If that man, one thought to be incorruptible, could be a traitor, then who else is hiding in the dark waiting to bring destruction down upon us…?" His unfinished thought drifted across the square, caught on the breeze, and set off to town in search of spies.

Seo had never felt so exposed. She tried to turn her head, to catch a glimpse of him, to see where he was, what he was doing, but the cage blocked her view.

"What are you looking for, sparrow? Or should I call you pigeon? You look like one in that cage."

Seo heard him move and flinched as he came into view. He walked past the cage and over to the brazier, warming his hands against the fire. "Not too cold yet, but I'm glad of this fire," he said. "It will be worse soon, though, maybe even tomorrow or the next day. I've heard the winter wind here can take the flesh off your bones." He reached into his pocket and took out a length of canvas, wrapping it around his right hand before pulling something from the fire. He turned, holding a metal rod, like a poker, the bottom third glowing red. "Are you cold, little pigeon?" He walked towards Seo, swinging the poker in front of him, the red-hot tip grazing the snow with a hiss and a burst of steam. He crouched down in front of Seo, the poker resting on the top of the cage, settling into a pose of complete stillness. Even from a distance she could feel the heat.

"I hate this place," said Nam. "You didn't expect me to say that, did you?"

Seo said nothing, her eyes fixed on the glowing tip of the poker.

"I probably hate it even more than you. But there is one thing that binds us together – we are both here because of you."

Seo shook her head. "I didn't do anything."

Nam coughed out a single laugh in a cloud of condensation. "No, no, you misunderstand me, Miss Ra. I am not suggesting you have any influence. Far from it. But that day at the museum, you stood within a few inches of our Supreme Leader. You, a traitor, and I did not stop it." His voice began to change, becoming quieter, deeper, coloured with hatred.

"And so, I was sent here. Me! Sent out of the capital to this cesspit because a girl listened to a radio and I didn't find out in time."

He stood so quickly that Seo barely saw it happen, drawing the poker back and stabbing it through the cage. Seo tried to twist out of the way, but there was nowhere to go and she screamed as the poker hit her belly with a searing pain. Her legs gave way, and she slumped down, the ropes cutting into her wrists.

"I was sure that if I got that ape Hwan to rough your friends up a bit, you would do something stupid. And you nearly did, didn't you? I could see it on your face." Nam began to circle the cage, stabbing the poker through at Seo's body as she squirmed in her cage, desperate to get away. "I didn't need a reason, of course. I can do whatever I like to you. But watching you break the rules makes it more entertaining for me."

He completed a full circle before tossing the poker to the ground in a cloud of steam. "You had it all, you know. A place in the capital, that remarkable voice I heard so much about. I bet you even dreamed of taking a holiday at Kijong-Dong, that beautiful town by the border." He squatted down beside her, his hair the colour of the snow. "Did you dream of Kijong-Dong?"

She nodded, too exhausted to care if it was the right thing to do.

"Well, your dreams are over. Mine are not. I will get out of here; I will go back to the capital. Maybe I'll send you a postcard from Kijong-Dong."

He stood, brushing the snow from his coat. "If you survive for two nights, I'll let you out." He lit a cigarette and took a drag, sending smoke through the side of the cage. "I have a feeling you will. I hope you do. I'd like to spend a lot more time with you, Miss Ra."

• • •

During the second night, when the wind had dropped a little and the snow fell in clean lines from steel clouds, Seo knew she would die. She found the knowledge in a corner of her mind, fully formed, as if someone had placed it there long ago. The pain from the burns inflicted by Nam had joined with the bone-breaking ache in her legs and the cuts from the ropes around her wrist, settling in a spot just below her heart. The pain didn't get worse anymore, but the spot felt more fragile every hour, like someone steadily pressing against a sheet of glass. Soon, she knew, the sheet would shatter, and her life would fly out of her chest in a million glittering shards.

Nam had not exaggerated about the wind, and although the walls around the execution site had given some protection, it had slashed at her face and torn at her clothes. Her hands, exposed above the top of the cage, had suffered the most. At first, she had been able to get some relief by clasping her fingers in the palm of her other hand, but as the pain had turned to numbness she had stopped. She could barely feel them now.

Images of her parents washed in and out of her mind, waves of memory that she thought she had forgotten a long time ago: sitting on her father's knee as he read from a book; her mother teaching her to sew; the time she had decided she wanted to be a singer.

Mr Chi's body still hung from the scaffold. The guards who took it in turns to watch her kept the brazier lit, so even at night she could see him, snow clinging to his frost-bitten body. She let her face hang down, not wanting it to be the last thing she saw.

She hardly noticed the sensation in her hands at first. It began as a soft stroking, slowly building in intensity. She wriggled her fingers and touched cloth, but it was gone again in a second. Then it came back, stronger this time, and she realised that someone was rubbing her hands, the feeling slowly returning to the tips of her fingers and spreading down. The rubbing stopped and she felt the cloth being wrapped tightly around her hands. She turned her head to look but she couldn't see anyone. "Who's there?"

"Shhh… Crusher gone," whispered a voice behind her. "But you can't make noise. He goes to the rest-hut and can hear-snitch if you make big noise."

Seo looked over at the brazier and saw the guard had gone. Her vision was blocked suddenly and she recoiled as someone thrust something through the front of the cage. She felt the warmth before she smelt the corn and she drank the soup before she could even think about how it got there, the bowl tilting with her mouth as the warmth flowed through her body, grains of rice catching in her teeth.

Finished, the bowl was pulled out of the cage and Iseul squatted down in front of her. "Some of your fingers are wintry. Too black. How many shifts?"

"Three," said Seo. She choked out the word, her throat aching with the effort. She couldn't quite believe that he was there or that he had bought her soup.

Iseul thought about this for a second. "Could be working,

could be dead-dead. The mush will help. If next shift you go back, should be working."

"How did you get here?"

Iseul shrugged. "It's not hard to march here, I know the way. Just can't be seen-snitched, that's all. I seen you last night when I try to sneak-carry corn."

"You came back?"

Iseul nodded.

"You'll get into trouble."

"You will see-snitch?"

"No, no. Of course not. I just don't want you to get in trouble, that's all."

A thump, like wood hitting wood, came from somewhere in the darkness behind the brazier. Iseul spun around, rising up slightly on his legs, head cocked to one side, his arms held out in front of him. He squatted motionless for what seemed like an age, then slowly relaxed, turning back to face Seo. "He is not marching. But soon." He inched closer to Seo. "The soup is warmly?"

"Very. Thank you."

Iseul nodded, apparently happy with this reply. "You show me the marching to Pyongyang."

If Seo could have laughed she would have. So that's why he had come. "I can't show you the marching to Pyongyang."

Iseul backed up a little and spat on the ground. "I carry soup for you. Inside is white gold. Good mush."

"I know, please don't be angry. It's just it will be very hard; I don't know how to get out."

"I know the marching out. You know the marching to Pyongyang."

Seo nodded, letting her wrists take the weight for a

moment to ease her legs. Even if she survived the night, the camp would kill her in the end. If Iseul knew a way out they had to try. "All right. I know the marching to Pyongyang. I'll take you there."

Iseul clapped. "Warmly mush with meat!"

"Is that why you came? Just so I could show you the way?"

Iseul thought about this for a moment, tapping the empty soup bowl against the side of his head. "I carry soup for you, you snitch the way to Pyongyang for me. This is warmly trade. But…"

"What is it?" asked Seo, worried about the look of confusion that had appeared on his face.

"Sometimes my head goes upside down and I want to carry soup because you are too much cold." He gave himself a hard knock with the bowl. "This is wintry trade."

"Thank you," said Seo. "That's very kind."

Iseul shook his head, like a dog shaking water from its coat. "No more upside down. Next time we will march together."

"How will I see you again?"

"Which place is your sleep-hut?"

Seo described the way as best she could, Iseul drawing out her directions in the snow with his finger. When she had finished he stared down at the drawing and then looked out across the camp. He grunted and nodded, quickly rubbing out the map. "I know the marching."

"Will you come?"

Before Iseul could answer, a flash of pain broke over one of Seo's burns and she cried out. Iseul leant towards her, his hand reaching into the cage. He slowly lifted up her shirt to reveal the burn near her waist and dropped it again with a hiss. "Which crusher is this?"

"Nam."

Iseul spat into the snow.

"You know him?"

"Everyone knows this new crusher. Harder shifts, longer shifts, no mush! He makes the whole world wintry." He sat back on his heels and crossed his arms, the snow-covered camp stretching out behind him.

Seo had never been more grateful for the company of someone else, for this strange boy from the darkest corner of the camp who had brought her food and warmed her hands. But the thought of dying still stayed as strong as ever. "Iseul."

He leant forward slightly.

"I'm afraid."

He looked at her, his head cocked to one side, and Seo saw the confusion in his eyes. He looked back past the brazier, as if trying to make his mind up about something, then raised himself up slightly and took two steps forward. He reached through the bars again and touched her hair, gently patting it with the tips of his fingers. "No need," he said in a calm whisper. "You have good mush now. Soon you will be in your sleep-hut and all will be warmly."

Another sound came from past the brazier and Seo felt the cloth being ripped off her hands as the guard stepped into the light. He warmed himself by the brazier, staring at Seo, then pulled a cigarette out and lit it. She hadn't even noticed Iseul go.

The guard settled onto his wooden stool, blowing smoke at the ground. Seo began warming her fingers in the palm of the other hand again, squeezing as tightly as she could, trying to keep the life in them that Iseul had brought with his soup and his words and the simple touch of his hand on her hair. Above her, the clouds parted a little, revealing a few scattered stars, pin-holes of light from another world. We won't march to Pyongyang, thought Seo, we'll march straight past it, all the way South, where the sleep-huts are strong and the mush is warmly. The guard's body seemed to flicker in front of her, then it slowly pulled itself apart, forming two guards on two stools. They stayed for a moment, seeming to hover a little above the ground, then tilted sideways and slowly faded into black.

FOURTEEN

Min sat by the fire, prodding the pot with his stick. Nari lay next to him, her eyes shut and her breathing calm, broken only by an occasional cough. Old Man Park stood nearby, his back to Seo. As she watched he turned slowly, holding something in his hands. He stopped and stooped down, peering at her. "She's awake!"

Min dropped his stick and rushed over, kneeling on the ground, gently resting his palm against her forehead. "The fever has broken."

Seo tried to raise herself up, but pain shuddered through her body and she slumped back down with a groan.

"Don't try to move," said Park. "Rest a while. I think the worst is over, but you are still too weak." He put his hand behind her head and drew her up a couple of inches, holding a bowl of warm soup to her lips. "Don't try and drink too much. That's right, just a little…"

"Seo!" Nari had woken up and crawled to her side, tears

on her cheeks. She lay down next to her, their heads touching. "You'll be all right now. We'll look after you."

Seo tried to speak but couldn't and Park raised his finger to his lips. "Don't try to speak. Nam let you out of the cage two days ago. You have been unconscious since then and…" He stopped, his voice cracking, and turned his face away for a moment. "But you'll be fine now." He carried on nodding for a few seconds after he had finished speaking, as if trying to reassure himself that it was true.

Seo tried to piece together what had happened. She remembered Nam's voice, harsh and mocking, then pain ripping through her as he pulled her out of the cage onto the snow. After that she couldn't find anything clear or solid, just fleeting glimpses of shadows and images that passed in and out of her mind. At times she thought she could hear voices, murmurs and whispers from far away, but when she tried to call out no sound would come. Then something else came back: Park standing above her, a knife in his hand, and his voice whispering, "*I'm sorry, I'm sorry.*"

She slowly raised her right hand, brushing past Nari, ignoring the pain, bringing it in front of her eyes. Someone had wrapped a grey-white bandage stretching from her wrist to her knuckles, with the tips of three fingers, streaked red and black, poking out from the frayed edge. It took her a second to realise what was wrong. She could feel her ring finger, the tip of it seemed to ache, but where it should have been was empty space, the bandage tied around a small stump. Tears welled up in her eyes, and she let her hand fall back down. Park knelt in front of her, his hand on her shoulder. "I'm sorry, Seo. There was too much damage and it became infected. It's why you had such a high fever." Seo nodded, holding his hand in hers.

"It's all right," she said, not sure if her voice was strong enough for him to hear.

"The others should heal, but it will take some time."

Seo drifted back into an uneasy sleep and dreams of the boy she had buried, only his face kept changing: first to hers, then Min's, then Nari's. Nam stood by the grave, running his hand through his hair, repeating the same phrase over and over: *did you dream of Kijong-Dong?*

She woke suddenly to find the hut quiet, her friends lying by the dying fire. Park had gone back to his own hut. She pushed herself up onto her elbow and felt a surge of dizziness. She stopped, taking deep, slow breaths, waiting for the feeling to subside before sitting up completely.

"Seo!" Min scrambled up, pushing his blanket away. "You shouldn't be up, you need to rest."

"It's all right. Is there some water?"

Min filled her cup from the jar and Seo took it, drinking in small sips, feeling the moisture penetrate her lips and tongue.

"I saved you some mush. Would you like some?"

Seo nodded and Min took the pot from the side of the fire and brought it over.

They sat in silence for a while, Seo nibbling tiny amounts of mush from the spoon. "It's good," she said.

Min smiled. "Moss and dried nettles," said Min. "Only the best."

Seo smiled back.

"We were so worried," said Min. "Nobody knew anything and we weren't allowed to go near you. When the guards brought you back..." He stopped, staring at the fire for a moment. "I was trying to calculate the temperature and how long you had been out in it and the possible effects that would have on somebody. I didn't know if you would live."

Seo reached out and put her hand on his shoulder. "I didn't think I would. In fact, I was sure I would die. Then something…"

"What?"

"Two people saved me. Two boys. One brought me soup and wrapped my fingers while I was in the cage. The other one left me this…" She lifted up her shirt, revealing the vest that the dead boy had been wearing when she took him to the graveyard. "Without those things I wouldn't have made it." She told Min about meeting Iseul on the way to the graves and how he had found her in the cage, but she didn't mention the pact to show him the way to Pyongyang; she would wait for a better time.

"I hope I get the chance to thank him," said Min. "But you know what Mr Park said about people who were born here…"

"I know. But I can trust him, I'm sure of that."

On the ground Nari coughed, a deep bark that resonated through the hut. She spluttered a little, swallowed and sank back to sleep.

Reaching out, Seo put her hand on Nari's hip, turning her eyes to Min.

"Her cough is getting much worse," said Min. "She finds it hard to catch her breath in the mine. Without you these past few days, it's been very hard pushing the trucks up."

"And you?"

Min hesitated for a moment, poking a stick into the fire, the light of the embers caught in the lens of his glasses. "Not so good. It gets harder every day. But we'll be all right."

"You're a lot smarter than me, Min. And I know that's not true."

"Lots of people survive the camps."

"And lots of people don't." Pain shot through her legs and she gasped, nearly dropping her bowl of mush.

"You need to rest. All the muscles in your legs are strained from the position they kept you in."

"If you don't work, you don't eat. Where are you getting the food for me from?"

Min turned away, prodding the fire again with his stick. "We've been smuggling some of ours back for you, as well as scavenging more."

Seo sighed, knowing how hard that must be on them. There wasn't enough in the first place, without having to give some away. "I'll go back to work tomorrow. It's not fair."

"Impossible. You need two more days' rest at least. The mine will kill you if you try and go back."

"Go back where?" Nari propped herself up on her elbow, her head resting on her hand. "Seo! You should be resting."

"So Min keeps saying."

Nari let out a series of explosive coughs, sending embers scattering across the hut. Min went quickly over, rubbing her back with the heel of his palm until the spasms subsided. Nari sat, gasping for breath, her hand on her chest until finally her breathing slowed. "That really hurts," said Nari. "And it really gets on my nerves."

The door opened with a shower of snowflakes and Seo caught the slash of the wind, sending her back to the cage and the pain. Park closed it behind him and walked quickly to the fire. "The temperature has dropped again. Tomorrow you must make sure you have plenty of wood. Everyone will be gathering it so…" He stopped, staring at Seo. "You should be resting!"

"The next person to tell me that…"

Park pulled something from his pocket and walked over, kneeling down beside her. "Lie back," he said. "I have to change your bandages." He slowly unwrapped a small roll of cloth bandage, greying and dotted with faded stains. Seo caught the whiff of something caustic, like a strong chemical. "Don't worry," said Park. "It's clean." He placed the bandages in Seo's lap and helped her to lie down, keeping his hand behind her head. "This might hurt a little." He began to peel back the bandage on her hands a centimetre at a time, glancing at her occasionally, concern in his eyes. Seo clamped her jaw together, ignoring the ant-bites of pain that ran across her hands. Finished, Park reached for the new bandages, but Seo shook her head.

"Wait. I want to see." Seo lifted her hands up in front of her face, turning them over slowly, as if she had never seen them before. She could move the stump from her missing finger and realised it looked like her father's, only smaller. If my dad can live with a missing finger so can I, thought Seo. "Will they always be black like this?"

"No," said Park. "They will heal and look normal again. But like I said, it will take some time."

"And this one?" Seo looked at the index finger on her left hand. It was darker than the rest, with a red streak running down the side; she could barely move it.

Park looked away for a second and sighed. "I don't know. If it gets infected, yes." He picked up the bandages and began to wrap them around her hands.

"Thank you," said Seo. She lay back, letting Park finish, listening to the voices of the wind. "Mr Park?"

"Yes?"

"Have you ever tried to escape from here?"

Park said nothing, concentrating on the bandages. Seo could feel Min and Nari staring at her, but she waited; she wanted to hear what he had to say.

Finished, he got up and walked towards the door. "Don't forget about the firewood tomorrow." He turned to go, then stopped. "Everyone who tries to escape from here dies. Everyone." And he walked out into the snow.

Min and Nari continued to stare at her, the smoke caused by the wind from the open door slowly thinning.

"Why did you ask him that?" said Nari, her voice a whisper.

"You know why."

"You're crazy."

"You heard Mr Park," said Min. "Besides, even if we could make it past the fence, where would we go?"

"South."

The hut slid back into silence. Min turned and looked at the door, Nari staring at Seo, her mouth open. "You've gone crazy."

"We can't stay here," said Seo.

"You want us to die?" A tear slid slipped down Nari's cheek, her voice trembling.

"No! I want us to live." Seo shuffled closer to the fire, the others doing the same, their faces flickering in the light from the flames. "We'll die here."

"Lots of people survive the camps," said Nari.

"And how many don't? Did you ever think there would be so many people locked up in here? And this is just one. How many others are there? How many people don't get out?"

"We can make it."

Seo nodded, looking directly into Nari's eyes. "Maybe we will. Maybe we'll survive this winter, and the next and the one after that. But eventually it will kill us. And let's say they do let us out before that happens. What then? Live as Hostile Class, mistrusted and shunned, having spent the last how many years snitching for food, snitching to live. We won't be who we were. Either way we die."

Nari nodded slowly, her teeth clenched. "It's that bloody radio."

"Nari, it's not—"

"It got us here and now you believe what we heard was true. They tricked you. They've made a fool of you! You believe all their lies and propaganda, and now you think we can just walk out of here into one of their stories."

"That's not it at all."

"Min," said Nari. "Please talk to her. You talk sense, she always listens to you. Please."

Min pulled his blanket around his shoulders, his eyes on the fire. "Something bothered me from the first time we switched on that radio."

"Me too!" said Nari. "We never should have done it."

"I don't mean that," said Min. "That's separate." He paused for a moment, staring into the fire. "All our lives they have told us the South is poor because of the Americans. So poor they have less electricity than we do. We don't have much food because we have to send it to them. So how can they have so much time to make those programmes? So much electricity to keep the signal going day after day?"

"That's why they don't have any!" said Nari. "They use it all for propaganda."

"That's possible," said Min. "But there is something else that's nothing to do with the radio."

"What?" said Nari.

"Mr Chi."

Seo felt the tears well up in her eyes, partly from the memory of his body hanging out in the cold, and partly at the relief that she wasn't the only one who realised how wrong that had been.

"We don't know what he'd done. You know you can't trust—"

"Stop it, Nari!" Seo took a breath, trying to ease the sudden flare of anger and the pain her raised voice caused. "How can you say that?" she said, struggling to keep her voice calm. "He was the most loyal man I've ever met, than any of us have ever met. You saw his face, he had no idea what was going on. He thought the guards must be spies."

"He never would have betrayed the state," said Min. "I'm sure of that."

"And you know why they brought him here instead of shooting him in the stadium? Because no one would have believed it. It would have been a lie too far even for the Party. This way they can say he ran off or defected or whatever rubbish they want."

"Seo, stop…" Nari's words morphed into a fit of coughing, but when Min went to help she pushed his hand away.

Seo waited until the coughing had subsided before speaking again, her voice calm and controlled. "To say Mr Chi deserved it is to say we deserve to be here. We listened to a radio, that's all."

Nari wiped her mouth with the back of her hand, taking in air in slow, shallow breaths. "But we did something wrong.

I know that, and I'm trying to make it right, but you can't and I don't know why. Now you want to try and escape and get us all killed."

"I wouldn't do anything to hurt you, Nari."

Nari looked at her, tears pooling in her eyes. "But you already have, Seo. You took the radio to Pyongyang. We told you not to, but you did anyway and now we're in here – because of you."

Seo's head spun, Nari's words chipping at her already cracked heart. She opened her mouth to speak but seemed to have forgotten all the words.

Nari lay down and pulled her blanket over her. "You and Min do what you want. But leave me out of it."

Silence settled over the hut, dampening any warmth the fire could create. Seo couldn't take her eyes off Nari, not quite believing what she had said. Min reached out his hand, touching her on the shoulder. "Don't listen to her. It wasn't your fault."

"Yes, it was," said Seo. "But I'm going to make it right."

FIFTEEN

"Hurry up," whispered Seo. "They'll miss us soon."

"It must be here somewhere," said Min. "Just give me a minute."

Seo strained her eyes in the darkness of the mine, trying to make out Min, but the lights had gone out at the end of the shift, leaving nothing but shades of black. Seo looked up the shaft towards the entrance, but she couldn't make out anything; the sounds of the other prisoners leaving for food and Ideological Struggle had faded. They'll be there soon, she thought, and then Nam will notice we're not.

She heard a thud and Min groaned in pain.

"Are you OK?"

"Fine. Just hit my head. I can't see a thing."

"Leave it. We'll look tomorrow."

"Just a little bit longer."

Seo held her eyes shut for a moment, then opened them wide, trying to make out something – anything – in the dark.

She heard the sound of metal scraping against metal and then Min was by her side. "Got it. Let's go."

They went as quickly as they could, stumbling over the tracks, Min half carrying, half dragging the metal axel. Most of the cart that had smashed on their first day in the mine had been cleared away, especially the wood, burned in the huts of those who had managed to smuggle it out. But the wheels and axels had been of no use, pushed to one side, waiting for a guard to tell them what to do with them, until Min realised an axel was just what they needed.

The area around the mouth of the mine stood deserted; everyone had moved on. "Hurry," said Seo. "We're going to be late."

Min took the axel to the far side, laying it down in scrub and kicking snow over the top. "Let's go."

They walked as quickly as they could without running, Seo glancing up at the guard tower, but he had his back to them, staring out across the camp. Coming around the corner to the hut, they quickened their pace, getting to the door just as the last prisoner went inside. Seo tried to hide her breathing as she sat down, taking in air through her nose, keeping her shoulders as still as she could. She felt a wave of dizziness and put her hand on the table to steady herself. Hwan stood by the mush pot, scratching his belly, but he didn't pay them any attention, and Seo allowed herself to relax as the prisoners lined up for their food.

Seo barely noticed Ideological Struggle. She went through the motions: two prisoners had fallen behind with bringing the coal from the face to the trucks, causing an unacceptable delay, and another had complained of being hungry. She didn't hear what she had done wrong that day but hung her head as the prisoners shouted their contempt and disappointment. All her mind was focused on Nari. She sat opposite, her face turned slightly away, avoiding Seo's searching eyes. Seo had tried to talk to her all day, but she wouldn't listen, pushing the trucks out of the mine in silence. Seo's pain had turned to resolve. Nari was right, it had been her fault, but she would make it right. They would get out and Seo would take them to the South.

As they had in the mine, Min and Seo hung back, making sure they were the last to leave, keeping their distance as they walked back past the mine. As they reached the spot where Min had hidden the axel they stopped, waiting until the other prisoners had walked out of sight.

"How are we going to get it back?" said Seo. "We can't just carry it."

Min glanced behind them, but no one had followed from the mush-hut, and he pulled the axel out from the shrub. "You're taller than me, so it will have to be you. Slide it down the side of your trousers and then cover it with your shirt. Use one hand to hold it and then lean on me. If anyone sees us they'll just think you're hurt."

Seo nodded, pushing the axel down her left leg. She had to hold it up slightly to stop it poking out of the bottom, but Min had been right: leaning against him it just looked as if she had hurt her leg.

They were about to set off when Seo stopped, snapping her head round in the direction of the trees.

"What is it?" whispered Min.

Seo strained her eyes, staring into the night. "I thought I saw someone."

Min looked over, scanning the trees. A rat scurried past,

vanishing on the other side of the path. "There's no one there," said Min.

"I could have sworn—"

"It's nothing. Come on, we need to get going."

They passed one guard on the way back, who looked at them for a moment and laughed. "No mush for you tomorrow if you aren't working, sparrow!" They bowed their heads, Seo vowing to make it to work the next day.

When they got back to the hut, Nari had curled up in her blanket, her back to them. Seo looked at Min, who touched her lightly on the arm. "It'll be all right. Give her time." He took the axel from Seo and stuffed it down a small gap where the floor met the wall, pulled off his glasses and polished the one still-intact lens. "All right, that's the first bit. Let's get some rest. The second will be much more dangerous."

• • •

The truck sat on a slight rise on the road leading towards the gates. Clouds covered the moon, casting the sleeping camp into grey shadow. The snow had frozen and Seo could feel the cold eating away at her shirt and vest as she lay on the other side of the road, watching and listening, her heart pounding against the frozen earth. Next to her Min shuffled, trying to get comfortable. "Shh," said Seo.

They had watched the truck for half an hour, waiting to see if the driver would return or whether he had a night-duty somewhere and wouldn't come back for it until the dawn. Half an hour seemed long enough, thought Seo, and she looked at Min, jerking her head in the direction of the truck. Min waggled a finger, indicating they should wait.

Somewhere near the gates a searchlight flashed into life, sweeping through the dark on the ground by the fence. It swung out towards them, the circle of light gliding up the road, and Min and Seo dropped their heads, trying to flatten themselves into the snow. Then, as quickly as it had come, the light vanished, leaving the dark and the cry of a night bird.

"We have to do this or go," whispered Seo. "We can't stay here. Either a guard or a prisoner will see us soon enough. And snitching on us will be worth extra rations for a month."

"Right," said Min. "If it's there, it'll be in the back. Ready?"

Seo nodded, and they crawled across the road to the truck. They stopped, Seo pushing herself against the wheel, not knowing if she would have the courage to stand to search the truck and risk being seen. She took a deep breath and raised herself to her knees, then clambered up and walked around to the back. Min grabbed the handle and pulled.

"Locked. We'll have to go, try again another night."

"No way," said Seo. "I'm not going through this again. There must be a way through the cab."

Before Min could object she went around to the side, pulled open the driver's door and crawled inside. Wire mesh separated the cab from the back of the truck, leaving a small gap between the wire and the side. Seo peered through, trying to make out the contents. In the far corner she saw what they needed, a crocodile clip for jump-starting in case the battery went flat, its red wire standing out against the jumble of tools and rags. She pushed her head through the gap, squeezing through one arm and then the other, trying to shuffle the rest of her body through.

"What are you doing?"

Seo could hear the urgency in Min's voice and felt his hand clamp around her ankle.

"Don't be stupid. You'll get stuck."

"There's one here," said Seo. "I can make it through."

Min began to tug on her leg, trying to pull her back.

"Stop it. I'm all right."

"You forgot your cigarettes!" The guard's words flew through the air like bullets, and Seo froze, the condensation from her breath hanging in the air in front of her. His voice told her he was very close and she had no way out. Go back for them, please go back for them…

"Bring them down!"

"No way. Come and get them."

"Lazy pig…" The guard's muttering faded away and Seo knew he had started the walk back.

"Get out now!" Min hissed the words, yanking on Seo's leg, but she wriggled free and fell into the back of the truck.

For a moment, Seo couldn't move, not quite believing what she had just done, the fear tensing every muscle in her body. She heard Min swear and the truck door being shut. Move, she thought, he'll only be a minute. She grabbed the crocodile clip and stuffed it down her shirt, shuffling on her knees towards the door. She could hear Min turning the handle, trying to force it open, and she pushed against it, but it wouldn't budge. A long thin strip of metal ran from the top to the bottom of the door, rattling every time Min tried the handle. She grabbed it, trying to push it upwards, but her hand slipped over the grease. In her mind she pictured the guard taking his cigarettes from his colleague, turning around, walking back towards the truck, his hand reaching for the door.

The fear gripped her tighter than ever, threatening to paralyse her, and she forced herself to breathe, trying to clear her thoughts. She felt around her with shaking hands and found a rag. Using it to grip the strip, she pulled up as hard as she could; the door swung open and she tumbled out into the snow.

"Get under!" Min grabbed her by the collar and they crawled underneath the truck just as the cabin door opened. Seo flattened herself against the ground as the engine coughed into life. The tyres skidded once, and a stinging pain ran across her cheek, then she was rolling and crawling across the road, back to the bushes where they had been hiding. They lay there, holding each other, Seo squeezing her eyes shut.

"If you ever do anything like that again," said Min, his voice coming in ragged gasps, "I'll kill you myself."

"If I ever do anything like that again," said Seo, not wanting to open her eyes, "please do."

SIXTEEN

Seo sat by the fire tying a piece of rag around her left boot. The sole had started to come away and she had to walk back from the mine with a boot full of snow. Nari had gone out for water as silently as she did everything, just shaking her head when Seo had offered to help. Min kept trying to reassure her that Nari would come around, that she didn't really blame her, but it had been three weeks and she had only spoken to Seo when it was absolutely necessary. Nari's cough got worse every day and Seo longed to comfort her, to fill the hole in her life where her best friend had once been.

Something thumped against the side of the hut and Seo dropped the rag, every nerve in her body instantly alert. On the other side of the fire Min stopped pacing and stared at the door. They waited in silence for it to be kicked down, for Hwan and some guards to rush inside, a prisoner behind them pointing and shouting. Seo counted to ten in her head and then allowed herself to relax. Min nodded to her and went back to his pacing, pinching his forehead with a finger and thumb, lost in thought. Since they had started to gather the things they needed, the thought of capture flickered constantly in her mind; every creak of a tree held a guard's shout, every breath of wind the whispers of snitches.

"It's no good," said Min, sitting down next to her, his shoulders slumped. "I can't think of any way to get the third piece."

"It's all right," said Seo. "We'll think of something."

"But to be sure it will work, it has to be copper. That would be hard to find at home, let alone here."

"We have to wait until the snow melts anyway, so there's plenty of time."

Min shuffled closer to the fire, running his hand down the front of his shirt. "I need to get a new shirt, this one is starting to fall apart."

"There's bodies on the paths nearly every day now. We should be able to find something for you."

Min nodded, picking up the stick he used to poke the fire, then fell backwards with a cry, ash and embers flying into the air.

Iseul sat on his haunches on the other side of the fire, his forearms resting on his knees, a small cloth bag dangling from his left hand.

"Iseul!" Seo stood up, not quite believing he was there. "How did you get here?"

"You showed me the marching and the crushers hide from the cold."

Min pulled himself back up. "Who are you?"

"This is Iseul," said Seo. "The one who brought me soup when I was in the cage."

Iseul nodded. "Good mush. I'm happy you are not dead-dead."

"Pleased to meet you," said Min.

Iseul stared at Min, slowly lowering his bag to the ground. Not taking his eyes off him, he slowly unwrapped the cloth, revealing five strips of dried meat. "Warmly meat," he said. "Better mush than the crushers will give you. You can carry it if you don't see-snitch…"

Min looked at Seo in confusion.

"It's all right," said Seo. "Min won't snitch. He's been helping me to get ready to march to Pyongyang."

Iseul clapped his hands. "When shall we march? After the next shift?"

Before Seo could answer, the door swung open and Park walked in, Nari only a step behind. Iseul hissed, springing to his feet and turning to face them. Park stared at him, a look of shock on his face, and for a moment nobody moved. Iseul ran towards the door, his head low, but Park grabbed him, holding him by his shirt, backing himself up against the door to close it. "So it's true," he said. "You've lost your minds."

Iseul struggled to get free, twisting his head round and burying his teeth in Park's hand. Park yelled and Iseul twisted away, running to the far side of the hut, knocking Min back to the floor. Nari cried out, moving closer to Park, her hands on her face. Iseul backed into the far corner, his fists raised and his upper lip curled up, showing clenched yellow teeth.

"Stop," said Seo, moving towards Iseul, her hand outstretched. "You'll have the guards here."

Park brought his injured hand to his mouth, sucking on the wound for a second. "You're the ones who'll bring the guards here. And it won't just be you they'll come for: me,

Nari, maybe the whole team in the mine. Plotting to escape with…" He faltered, as if looking for the right word, gesturing over to Iseul. "With one of *them*. They'll shoot us all."

"He will see-snitch," said Iseul, spitting the words towards Park. "No mush, no shifts, into the cage! The crushers will carry white gold for him for this big snitch."

"You little rat…" Park took a step towards Iseul, his hand raised, but Seo grabbed him by the arm.

"Please," she said. "You don't understand. Just listen to me for a moment."

Park looked at her, his fist still raised. "There's nothing I don't already know. You're not the first to be tricked by one of them. He'll be bathing in mush for this one."

Min pulled himself up from the floor for the second time and pushed his glasses back up his nose. "I really think you should listen to Seo. I don't think it's as simple as that."

Park took a deep breath and slowly lowered his arm. "All right. I need to think how to get you out of this one anyway." He moved back towards the door, his eyes on Iseul. "You're not going anywhere."

"Come and sit down, Nari," said Seo. But Nari just shook her head and stood next to Park, doubling over for a moment as a cough ripped through her.

As she had with Min, Seo explained the night in the cage to Park, of how he had bound her hands and brought her soup, had given her the hope that they might make it out alive. When she had finished, Park took a step away from the door and pulled off his cap, scratching at his bald patch for a moment. "Well, I've never heard of anyone doing that, I must admit," he said. "They could have shot him on the spot."

Seo nodded, smiling over at Iseul. "I trust him. I really do."

"Well, you shouldn't," said Park. "He'll help you one day and then club you over the head the next. And I told you before, everyone dies who tries to get out of this place. You need to stop whatever it is you're planning right now. You can bet somebody knows or at least suspects something already, and whatever the plan is, it's been tried before."

"Tell him about the place the crushers don't go. Where we can get through the fence without being seen," said Seo. Iseul shook his head, pointing at Park.

"You still don't get it, do you!" said Park. "Everyone in this place is a guard. They starve us for a reason: so a man would sell his grandmother for a handful of rice. And even if you did make it to the fence, it's got three thousand volts running through it! You saw what happened to that woman who tried to make a run for it."

"I think I know a way around that," said Min. "We have most of what we need already."

Park pressed his fingers to his temples and took a deep breath. "Here's what's going to happen: you're going to get rid of whatever stuff you've been getting hold of and you're never going to talk about it again." He turned to Iseul. "And we need to get rid of you too."

Seo felt a sudden rush of anger, jumping up and putting herself between Iseul and Park. "Didn't you listen to anything I told you? If it wasn't for him I'd be dead."

"It's because of him you will be soon."

"You are such a coward."

Park looked like he had just been slapped across the face.

Seo took half a step back, shocked by what she had said. "Maybe I will die, but it will be on my terms. I'd rather die on the fence or freeze in the hills than rot in that mine working for them."

"You bitch." Nari took a step forward and Seo could feel the anger radiating off her. "Mr Park has done everything for us. We wouldn't have survived this far if it wasn't for him. How can you talk to him like that? Why do you—" A fit of coughing cut her off and she doubled over, covering her mouth with her hand then bringing it away speckled with blood. She stared at it for a second, then her eyes rolled back in her head and she crumpled into Park's arms.

Min jumped up and helped lay Nari down on her blanket. Seo grabbed her own blanket and stuffed it under her head. "Nari," she said, tears running down her cheeks, "can you hear me?"

Park put his hand on her forehead. "High fever. She needs warmth and plenty of water."

"What about the blood?" said Seo.

Park thought for a second. "I'm not sure. It might just be bronchitis. Or it could be worse. I'll see what I can find to help, but it is late now. I might not be able to get back until the morning."

"It's all right," said Min. "We can look after her."

"We still need to deal with him, though." Park turned to the corner where Iseul had been standing. He had vanished. "Damn."

"It's all right," said Seo. "I know you don't trust him, but please trust me. He wants to get out of this place so badly, I know he won't say a word."

Park grunted. "We'll see." He stood up and walked towards the door.

"Mr Park?" said Seo.

He stopped, his hand on the doorframe.

"I'm sorry. About what I said. I didn't mean it."

Park hesitated for a moment, then gave her a brief nod and vanished into the night.

Nari woke a few hours later. Seo lay next to her, unable and unwilling to sleep, wiping the sweat from her friend's face. Min lay nearby, his glasses hanging crooked on his nose, sleeping as silently as he always did.

"Are you there, Seo?"

"I'm here, of course. Shhh. Try and sleep."

"What's wrong with me?"

"Mr Park thinks it's bronchitis. Don't worry, we'll get you better. It's my turn to be the nurse."

"It's all right if I die."

"Stop it. You're not going to die." Seo pushed in a little closer, holding her friend tightly, feeling her fragile bones under the layers of rags. "I'm going to look after you."

"I'm sorry for telling Mr Park what you were doing. I was just so scared."

"It's all right. We would have told him anyway. I want him to come with us."

Nari nodded. "That's good." She shivered, the last word clattering out through her trembling jaw. "I need to tell you something. I was hoping I never would, but I can't bear it anymore."

"Don't worry. You can tell me anything."

"I can't go back to the world. It's better if I die in here."

"Don't talk like that. You—"

Nari cut her off with a shake of her head. "It's not your fault we're here. I'm sorry I said that; I wanted someone to blame. That way I didn't have to feel so guilty, but then I saw what they did to Mr Chi and I knew I couldn't hide from it anymore."

"Don't say that."

Nari turned her face away. Her voice was barely a whisper, each word squeezed out of pain. "Do you remember they made you say it was your singing teacher who made you listen to the radio?"

"That's right. But it was a lie."

"They made me say it was my dad."

The words gripped Seo's heart and she hugged her friend as close as she could, desperately trying to will away her pain.

"I think I killed my daddy."

SEVENTEEN

Seo had always known hunger. It had been part of her life for as long as she could remember, like washing or walking to school. But as their supplies ran out, it took on a new form, something living within her, a parasite gnawing at her flesh, eating her from the inside out. Work in the mine had become almost impossible. The carts seemed to get heavier every day, the shaft a metre longer, the bowls of mush an inch shallower. Twice Seo had collapsed at the top, unable to go on, the world around her spinning as she struggled to breathe. Yet somehow they managed the quota, and as the days passed she realised two things held her together. The first was Min: he always had a gentle word, a rational thought, pushing the carts with a silent refusal to give in. The second were the words Nari had spoken: *I think I killed my daddy*. They fuelled a rage in Seo that fought back the hunger and the cold. And she knew if she ever met the men who had done such a thing to her friend, she would split their skulls open with a rock.

Prisoners invented wilder and wilder stories at Ideological Struggle in the hope of winning favour and food from the guards.

"*I saw prisoner 347 eating rice while working! He must have stolen it from the guard hut!*"

"*424 is a spy! He is sending messages to the Americans though the fence!*"

"*384 is plotting to kill a guard! I heard her myself!*"

Mostly the guards didn't take these seriously, Hwan especially, relishing the theatre of it, often laughing and goading the others to match the seriousness of the crimes. Occasionally a prisoner would be dragged out and beaten, an extra spoonful of mush given to the snitcher, but mostly they were ignored. Seo and Min kept their confessions simple and plausible, focusing on their own failings. Over time, this seemed to bore Hwan, and he focused his attentions elsewhere.

She had not seen Nam since his visit to her in the cage. Every day she looked for him, expecting some new punishment or trick to get her in trouble, but he never came, and although she slept better at night for his absence, something about it troubled her. He didn't seem like a man who wouldn't follow through with a threat.

Iseul had not come back. Seo worried that he had been frightened away for good and she prayed that his will to escape would be strong enough to overcome his fear. They needed to know where it was safe to get through the fence, but they needed to find the copper wire as well.

Nari hadn't been able to work for a week, her fever spiking at night, leaving her shivering and coughing in her blanket. They smuggled out as much food for her as they could, but it was risky work, and sometimes they were just too hungry to be able to do it, leaving them to walk back to the hut, shame at failing their friend pushing their spirits even lower. A faint rash appeared on Seo's arm and she kept it hidden from the others. She knew it was pellagra, the disease Park had warned them would take hold if they didn't have enough protein. She knew it wouldn't become dangerous for a long time yet, but it added to the need for them to get out. Park came as often as he could, bringing what he could spare, but the winter took its toll on him too, pinching the skin on his cheeks, forcing his long stride into a shuffle.

"Where will you go if you get past the fence?"

It was the first time Park had made any mention of their plan to escape since the night Iseul had come. He sat by the fire nibbling at a piece of dried rat, staring at the wall, as if he could see some faraway place through the concrete and the falling plaster.

Min looked at Seo and raised his eyebrows. She nodded, wanting to talk to Park about it but unsure where the conversation would go, the guilt at calling him a coward still fresh.

"We'll head north," said Min. "I've heard there are people near the border who can help you get across the river into China."

"I've heard that too," said Park. "I've also heard there are people who will take what you have and hand you over to the army."

Seo's hopes sank. He was going to try and talk them out of it again.

Park took a tiny bite of his meat, rolling it around his mouth before swallowing. "I've also heard that once you get across the border, the Chinese will sell you back."

"It's the only way I've ever heard to get out," said Min.

Park reached into his shirt and pulled out a small piece of paper. He unfolded it carefully and placed it on the floor next to him. "Have you heard of Kijong-Dong?"

"Of course," said Seo. "It's on the border with the South. I used to dream of being able to go there. They say it's the most beautiful town in Korea."

"Yes, I've heard that too," said Park. "But I actually did go there."

Min shuffled a little closer to Park. "You've been to Kijong-Dong? What was it like?"

"If you get past the fence, you can find out yourself. It wasn't finished back then and was mostly empty so I couldn't really tell you." He picked up his piece of paper again and handed it to Min. It was a map, drawn freehand in pencil, some of the lines beginning to smudge, but the outlines of buildings and streets still clear.

"I used to be in a special unit of the army. The official name is the Special Engineering Corps, but everyone just called us the Tunnel Rats. The border between us and the South is four kilometres of barbed wire and land mines. A mouse can't cross it without being blown up or shot. The Tunnel Rats dug under the border with the South for spies to cross, and maybe even for an invasion. Two of the tunnels were huge, big enough to drive a tank through. But the bigger they were the easier it was for the soldiers in the South to find. They just blew them up or poured concrete into them from their end. Pointless really."

He took another bite. "It's how I got the job as supervisor for the mine. I know how to work underground. Anyway, it soon became clear the tunnels weren't viable and the whole idea was scrapped. The tunnels the South didn't find usually caved in anyway." He reached a finger over the side of the map and stabbed into the bottom right corner. "But this one was the smallest and the longest. I supervised the digging myself."

"But that looks like it's inside a building," said Min.

"It is."

"Wouldn't it have collapsed by now like the others or been found?" Seo couldn't take her eyes off the corner of the map, not quite daring to believe that they might be able to just walk into the South.

Park nodded. "That is possible, but I'm not so sure. We dug it deep and strong, and very few people knew about the tunnels. After they abandoned the project, people largely forgot about them. We stayed in Kijong-Dong for some months afterwards, manning the propaganda speakers and taking care of the town. Before they moved us out I went to see the tunnel. I was proud of it and disappointed they had scrapped them." He lifted his hands, turning his head up towards the others, a smile growing on his face. "We had concealed the entrance so well even I had a hard time finding it. But there it was, my masterpiece, still intact. Only the last section left unfinished."

Min looked down at the map, nodding to himself, lost in thought, his thumb stroking the spot that marked the entrance to the tunnel.

"But there is one other reason I think it's still there." Park dropped the words out like someone too proud of a secret to keep it anymore. "We were supposed to keep a record of which tunnels had been found or destroyed and which hadn't. If they hadn't, we were supposed to do it ourselves.

We couldn't have the Americans using our own tunnels against us. Then an official from Pyongyang arrived and told us to mark it down as destroyed." He gave a short laugh at the memory and tossed the last scrap of meat into his mouth. "I'm not sure why he asked me to do that. But I was happy. I would have hated to have blown it up after all that work."

"Perhaps they thought they'd need it one day?" Seo kept her voice as still as she could, not wanting the question to sound like an accusation.

"Maybe. Everyone I knew down there has vanished. And I'm in here."

Nari coughed, breaking Seo's daydream of walking through a tunnel into the South. She smoothed out her blanket and rested her palm on Nari's forehead.

"She doesn't feel so hot tonight."

Park leant over and checked. "You're right. This is very good news." He took a deep breath, as if having finally made a decision, and reached into his bag, pulling out smaller bundles. He opened the first one and poured seven white pills into his hand. "These are aspirin. They will help bring Nari's temperature down. A few hours before you leave give her two, then two more about three hours later." He handed the pills to Seo, who took them without a word, staring at them as if they had just fallen from the sky. The second bundle contained strips of dried meat, more than Seo had ever seen at one time. "You must ration these very carefully." Min took them as if afraid they might crumble away in his hands if he moved too quickly. Park paused at the third bundle, a smile on his face. "I'll owe the supervisor in the machine shop for the rest of my life for this one." He held up a coil of wire like a trophy. "It had to be copper, right?"

"That's right," said Min, his voice barely a whisper.

Seo couldn't take her eyes off Park. She knew it would have cost him everything he had to bring them these things.

"That little rat hasn't snitched yet, which means he probably won't, and his belly will bring him back the first chance he gets. When he comes, you go that night. Don't wait."

"What about the snow?" said Min. "Shouldn't we wait until spring?"

"Nari looks like she's getting better. But she won't survive the mine. Her lungs are not strong enough and none of us will survive if she can't work. You have to get out." He picked up his bag and stood. "Which way you go is up to you. But the Chinese border is far and very dangerous. It's only a few days to the South from here. I'd trust the tunnel."

He walked towards the door.

"Come with us," said Seo. "Please. I don't want to think of you stuck in here."

Park put his hand on the door, leaning his weight against it and shaking his head, and Seo thought he had never looked so old. "I can't leave. I know what you think about me for that."

Seo stood. "No, I don't. I'm so sorry, I never meant—"

"If I leave with you, whether we make it or we die, I'll never see my home again. I've survived two winters; I'll survive this one as well. But I'm old now. They won't keep me here much longer, I'm no threat to them. I want to see the hills I played in as a boy and the town hall I married my wife in. I want to die at home."

"We'll never forget what you've done for us," said Seo.

Park nodded and went to leave, then stopped. "I hope

you make it. I don't know what the South is like, but it can't be any worse than here and I've heard stories, the same as you. I'm not sure what to believe, but I'll always remember asking my mother about the war. She said she remembered the Americans arriving in our town. You must have been very afraid, I said. I'd always been told the Americans had killed everyone on sight during the war. She just laughed and said, 'I never saw them do anything like that. They gave us all chocolate and chewing gum.'"

Seo stared at the door for a long time after he had left, the aspirins for Nari still in her hand, picturing his mother skipping alongside a tank as the Americans threw her chocolate, trampling on any lingering doubt she may have had. She glanced at the map and the wire, watched Min carefully divide the meat into three piles, and felt a light begin to grow in her soul once more, lit by the goodness of Old Man Park.

EIGHTEEN

The guard pissed forever, humming an old folk song out of tune while he filled the air in front of him with a geyser of steam. He had caught them unawares, stepping out of the mist without a sound. Only Iseul had seen him (or sensed him?) and managed to get them behind a rock before he spotted them.

Hurry up! Seo had crouched awkwardly and the muscles in her calf began to tighten, cramp squeezing its way up to her knee. Nari held a piece of rag over her mouth with both hands, tears forming in her eyes from the effort not to cough. Min lay next to Iseul, his eyes fixed on the guard, his breathing slow and shallow.

Iseul had arrived that night, his face peering in through the door. "The old snitch is in his sleep-hut?"

It had taken Seo a few seconds to stop laughing, loving the relief as it flooded through her. "Are you ready to go?" she said.

Iseul clapped his hands, a smile spreading across his face. "Let's march!"

Despite his enthusiasm he had insisted they wait until the early morning, two hours before dawn. It was the quietest time, he said. "Everything is hushly. All the crushers are hiding."

The guard signalled he had finished with a burst of flatulence that sounded like a mine cart freewheeling down the tracks. The last note of the folk song vibrated in the air for a second, followed by a 'zip', and he walked back the way he had come.

Seo slowly stretched out her leg, her muscles wanting to crack, and rubbed her calf as hard as she could. Iseul signalled they should continue, and they crept out past the rock, following the ditch that separated the road from the cornfields. They passed the tower the guard must have come from, the top lost in the mist, only a yellow glow of an interior light showing anything was up there at all. Iseul led them further through the camp than Seo had been before. They passed the graveyard and the rock where she had first met him, the lumber mill and the execution site, and took a winding path up towards the mountain. A steady hum began to surround them, and Seo knew they had come close to the fence. They didn't see any more guards, and Iseul moved through the dark effortlessly, dropping into ditches, skirting huts and trees, providing a route that kept them as far away from the towers as possible while keeping them on a steady path towards the only other place in the camp where the guards never went.

They stopped in front of a clump of fir trees, a path twisting down and away to the right. "That march is the stone-carry.

Hard shift, cold shift, carry stone from the mountain. But I find this warmly place. No crushers, good rest."

The fence ran onto the mountain, the final pole visible against the rock. In front of them a jumble of massive stones had formed a natural wall against the path.

"Landslide," said Min.

Iseul clambered up onto the first boulder, dropped down and vanished from sight.

Seo followed. Behind the first boulder was a space just big enough for one person to stand, but for a moment she couldn't work out where Iseul had gone. She reached around the rock in front of her and squeezed her body through, her clothes snagging. For a horrible moment she thought she was stuck, then she pulled herself through and found herself in a small clearing, bordered by the rocks, the fence and the side of the mountain.

"This is good," said Min. "No one will be able to see us."

"I show the marching here," said Iseul, his arms folded, staring defiantly at Seo. "Now you show the marching past the fence."

"Are you ready?" she asked Min.

"I have everything we need, but we have to clear the snow first."

Nari wanted to help, but Seo wouldn't let her, making her sit on a small rock with her back to the mountain. "You're not strong enough yet," she said.

"Are we crazy?" said Nari.

"I think we're about to find out."

The landslide had formed a natural shelter from the wind and the snow lay thin and patchy. Using their hands, they cleared a pathway from the fence to the far side of the clearing, ensuring there was enough space from them without any snow.

"Snow's made of water," said Min. "Water conducts electricity very well."

Together, they drove the cart axel into the ground about three feet from the fence, Min measuring the distance with the jump leads to ensure they would reach. He pulled out the copper wire from his bag and carefully wound it in a spiral from the top to the base of the axel, clamping one end of the jump leads to the centre.

Iseul squatted down next to the pole, running his hand over the wire. "This one can beat the fence?"

"Yes," said Min. "It can beat the fence."

Iseul shrugged and went over to sit next to Nari.

"All right," said Min. "I think we're ready. Get as far back as you can."

"What about you?" Seo touched his arm, her body filling with anxiety.

"I should be fine."

Without thinking, Seo leant over and pecked him on the cheek. Min brought his hand to his face as if he had just been slapped, his face boiling to crimson.

"Sorry…" Seo felt her own cheeks redden and took a step back. "Just wanted to wish you luck."

Min mumbled something, which could have been 'thanks', then took a deep breath and walked towards the fence.

"You know, I'm almost tempted to let you do it, just to see if you survive or not."

Seo's body went rigid. She didn't need to look to know who had spoken. She heard Iseul hiss and Nari let out a sharp cry. Min stood with the jump leads in his hands, despair in his eyes.

"Turn around, sparrow."

Seo turned, short, shuffling movements, the strength draining out of her body, sucked out by the fear.

Nam stood by the rocks, a rifle in his hands and a smile on his face. "Kneel down, all of you. In a line."

They did as they were told: Min, Seo, Nari and Iseul at the far end. He stared at the space behind Nam and leant forward slightly. Nam snapped his rifle up, staring down the sights at Iseul. "Don't even think about it, rat." Iseul moved his hands slowly to his head and sat back on his feet.

Nam lowered his rifle slightly, sweeping it across all of them. "Next person to move gets shot." For a moment, he said nothing, staring at each of them in turn, creating a silence that wrapped itself around Seo, gripping her throat, forcing the air out of her lungs.

"How did you think no one would know?" Nam's voice became a sneer. "I knew you were up to something when one of the prisoners saw you hide the axel. No one can fart in this place without me knowing. I thought I would take you then and there, throw you all in the cage. But then I realised this was my opportunity. You had to be trying to escape somehow, and when the jump leads went missing from a truck I knew it had to be you. Took me a while to find where you had hidden them, though. And when the rat here sneaked across to see you I knew you were trying to escape and all I had to do was wait." He cleared his throat and spat the phlegm on the ground. "Hwan told me it was against the regulations to let you share the same hut. But I knew if I kept you all together it would be the best way to let you cook up some stupid idea. And you have excelled yourselves."

No wonder it had been so easy, thought Seo. He had let them. She remembered Park questioning why they had a hut together, and now she knew. She wondered if she could reach him in time. There were four of them. Even if he managed to shoot her, the others could overpower him, perhaps, and make it out. Guilt ran through her body like oil. They had been caught and it was her fault again. Everything had been her fault.

"You have given me my chance," said Nam. "I'm catching five prisoners in the act of escaping – I'm surprised to see the old man isn't here. But I'll deal with him later. This will give me my promotion, maybe even my way out. Get my job back in Pyongyang, where I can raise my family far away from your stench. But it had to be mine alone. I'm not sharing this with anyone." His face broke into a smile. "One of you at least has to die here, though. Makes me look more heroic if there are signs you tried to fight. The rest can swing in front of the entire camp."

Seo knew then that she must do it. He would kill one of them, and she wanted it to be her. Min would know what to do. She closed her eyes and saw her parents. Her mother in her best dress, her father with his arms around her, and the strength began to flow back into her legs. I can do it. I'll be quick enough.

She opened her eyes and stared at Nam, tensing every muscle in her body.

"Don't stare at me! I guess it will be you that doesn't make it. Although I was looking—"

A dull thud filled the air and a red mist erupted out of the back of Nam's head, forming a brief halo over his white hair. He took half a step forward, his body jerking. A gunshot sounded and Seo felt the bullet fly over her head and hit the rock behind her. Nam's eyes rolled up in his head and he fell forward onto his face, lying with his feet twitching, blood pooling around his head.

Park stood behind him, still holding the rock he had used.

Seo fell forward onto her hands, gulping in air by the lungful. Next to her Nari began to cry. Seo pushed herself up and put her arms around her.

"No time," said Park. "They would have heard that shot on the other side of the camp." He dropped the rock and picked up Nam's rifle. "Min, quickly. There's no time to lose." Min didn't move, staring at Nam's body. "Min!"

Min started, as if waking from a deep sleep.

"Are you ready?" said Park.

"Yes," said Min. He scrambled up and grabbed the jump leads.

"You," said Park, pointing at Iseul and then at Nam. "You know what to do."

Iseul crawled over to Nam's body and began stripping it, starting with his boots and moving up. In the distance, the morning siren sounded.

For Seo, everything seemed to be happening beyond her control. She helped Nari to the far side of the clearing, but the world had taken on an unreal edge, like living in a painting where the colours weren't quite right.

"Let's go, Min," said Park. "No time to lose now."

Min walked to the fence, his arm outstretched, his hand clamped around the handle of the jump lead, forcing the clip as wide as it would go.

Sparks flew from the fence and Min fell backwards, as if some giant fist had punched him in the stomach. A sound like a clap of thunder filled the clearing, the rubber casing of the jump leads bursting into flames.

"Min!" Seo jumped up and rushed to her friend. He lay on the floor gasping for breath, his right hand burned and blackened.

"I'm all right," he said. "I'm all right."

"The guards will be up here in minutes," said Park. "First the shot, now this. Time to go." He put down the rifle and walked to the fence, pulling two of the cables apart to make room for them to squeeze through. Nari went first, then Iseul carrying Nam's clothes wrapped up in the coat, Min and lastly Seo. When they were all through Park let the cables go with a twang.

"What are you doing?" said Seo. "Come on."

Park shook his head. "They'll catch us all. If I stay, they will think it was just me, for a day at least. Besides, I'm going to give them something more to worry about than just escaped prisoners. You can be far away by then."

"No," said Seo. "They'll kill you. If you come, you'll live. Not at home, but it has to be better."

"None of us will make it if we all go. I've had my life. Now you can go and have yours." He slid the bolt on the rifle with practised ease. "Fly now, my sparrows. Try and keep close to the trees."

"Please come with us." Seo choked out the words, not wanting to believe what he was going to do.

Park just smiled, resting the butt of the rifle on his shoulder, and began to sing an old army song that Seo had heard a hundred times as the soldiers marched past.

I'll see you at the docks when the boats are ready.

Seo felt Min tugging at her arm. "We have to go."

Lace up your packs, keep your rifles steady.

Park turned and walked back across the clearing, vanishing through the rocks, his voice still clear in the morning mist.

Say goodbye to my sweetheart for me.

Min half pulled, half dragged Seo away from the fence, Iseul leading them away from the deeper snow.

A shot rang out, then another, followed by a scream.

Will I ever kiss her again under the maple tree?

The air seemed to erupt in gunfire, shouts and screams and Seo turned, running with the others around the side of the mountain towards the woods, the gunfire fading away, leaving only their ragged breathing and the screams of the wind.

NINETEEN

Min stopped, his shoulders heaving as he tried to catch his breath. He pointed to a group of hills in the far distance. "That's south," he said, gasping out the words. "Even if there are no stars at night or the cloud is too thick to see the sun, we just have to head in the direction of those hills and we know we are going in the right direction."

Seo looked back across the way they had come, their footprints standing out like coal stains on a white sheet. They had hiked for at least three hours, the sirens fading away and the last watchtower dropping behind the horizon at what seemed an age ago, but every second she expected to hear barking dogs and the shouts of guards as they ran towards them with their rifles raised.

Nari had managed to walk unaided for a while, much longer than Seo could have hoped for, but now her arms hung around Seo's neck, her body weight pulling them both down. Seo adjusted her footing, putting her arm around Nari's waist, and tried to hoist her upright. She raised her head, stared at Seo and said, "Mr Park…" Then her eyes closed and she slumped backwards.

"Hold her," said Min. "Don't let her fall into the snow."

They half carried, half dragged Nari towards a small cluster of trees, Min and Iseul brushing the snow away as best they could before sitting her up against one of the trunks.

Nari moaned, her teeth chattering, waving a hand in front of her face as if trying to brush something away. Seo took her hand and held it tight, pulling it towards her chest, waiting for the moaning to subside.

"Bring me Nam's coat," said Seo. She draped it over her friend, tucking the collar in under her chin. She pressed her hand against her forehead and looked at Min. "She's very hot again."

"How many pills do you have left?"

"Only four."

Min thought about this for a moment. "Better give her two now and let her rest for a while."

"No resting!" said Iseul. "Crushers will be marching soon! Double-time!"

"We can't move her, Iseul. She's too sick."

Iseul looked at Nari for a moment, then shook his head. "Too wintry. Will be dead-dead on the next shift."

Seo jumped to her feet, her hand raised, anger surging through her. "Stop it! Don't say that!"

"Relax." Min stood between them, one hand on Seo's arm, slowly pushing it down. "We can't argue with each other. Not now, of all times." He turned to Iseul. "Can you keep watch for us?"

Iseul looked at Seo for a moment, his head cocked slightly to one side as if trying to work something out, then spat on the ground and walked to the edge of the trees. He squatted down, staring back in the direction they had come.

Seo let herself fall back against the trunk of the tree. "I'm sorry, I shouldn't have got so angry."

"It's not his fault. It's the camp. It's all he's ever known."

Seo nodded. "I know."

"But he's right about one thing. We can't stay here too long. They might not be looking for us yet, but they will be soon."

"She can't walk, Min. And none of us will get very far if we try and carry her."

"I need to rest and think for a moment."

Seo took the parcel of food from their bundle and gave Min two strips of the dried rat meat. She took the same over to Iseul, wanting to apologise for shouting. He looked up at her, confused and hurt.

"You are too much angry. But I can't understand."

She squatted down next to him. "I'm not angry, Iseul. I'm sorry. I'm just feeling… upside down."

Iseul nodded, as if he knew exactly what she meant. She handed him the meat and he took it, smiling, then pointed out in front of him before tapping the side of his head. "Good see-snitching."

"Thank you." She left him scanning the horizon, chewing on his food, and sat down next to Nari. She pushed in close, trying to share the warmth of her body with her friend. She felt her eyes grow heavy, and let them close, giving in to sleep.

The noise of breaking wood woke her, and she sprang to her feet, every nerve in her body instantly awake.

"Sorry," said Min, dragging a tree branch towards her. "I didn't mean to wake you."

"It's fine. I got a fright, that's all."

"I had an idea."

Together they broke off three more branches, each about a metre and a half long. Min tore strips from Nam's shirt and used them to bind them together, leaving the twigs and leaves intact to provide some cushioning. Nari had stopped shivering, but still didn't respond. They carried her to the sledge and laid her down, Seo making sure that Nam's coat covered her as much as possible.

They took it in turns to drag the sledge, rotating around with one person walking a little way ahead, keeping lookout. It worked well, and despite the jarring, Nari didn't show any signs of distress.

Their route took them across mainly open ground, scattered with copses, but they hadn't seen any sign of a town or village, not even a small farm. Seo began to realise how isolated the camp was, cut off from the rest of the country by more than its fences. But if Park had been right, they were only twenty miles from Pyongyang and 140 miles from the border. She glanced back at Min and Iseul, dragging Nari through the snow – it might as well be a thousand.

"We need to find somewhere to sleep for the night," said Min. "We can't stay out in the open like this. I can feel the temperature dropping already."

"I'll take over," said Seo. "Iseul, can you look ahead for us?" Iseul nodded and trotted off, heading towards the nearest clump of trees.

Min gently lowered the sledge. "I just want to rest for a moment. Just a few seconds."

He had turned pale, his hands shaking as he brought them to his mouth, trying to breathe some warmth into them.

"Here," said Seo, taking his hands and rubbing them with her own. "Better?"

"Much. Thank you."

"Don't you get sick, too." As she said the words, she knew they couldn't have got this far without him, that they wouldn't get any further without him. "Do you think Nari will die?"

Min looked away, rubbing his sleeve across his eyes. "If we can't find proper shelter soon, then there is a high probability, yes."

Despair hit her so quickly, she didn't have a chance to brace herself for it, tearing through her body like a knife, cutting out any positive thoughts, any sign of hope. Nari had been right: she had just brought them out of the camp to die. At least she had walls and fire before; now they had nothing but snow, wind and some dried rat. She fell to her knees, wishing she could cry, to wash the feeling out through her tears, but none came, and she felt she must have used them all long ago.

"What is it, Seo?" said Min, dropping down behind her. "What's the matter?"

"Nari was right. This is my fault. I've killed Mr Park, and I'm going to kill Nari. We should have stayed in the camp."

"Enough!" The anger in Min's voice shocked Seo, and she jerked back, staring into his face. "Mr Park was the bravest man I ever met. He died doing what he felt was right, and I'll forever be in his debt. We're doing that too – what's right. Nari will die if we don't get her medicine and she's not going to get that in the camp. If we'd stayed Nam would have killed you – very slowly, one trip to the cage at a time. I'd rather die out here than watch you both die in there."

Seo nodded. "I'm sorry…"

"Now get up." Min held out her his hand and helped her to her feet. "We're going south. We are going to make it to the border and get out using Mr Park's tunnel. Say it."

Seo willed the strength back into her body and mind, picturing Mr Park, rifle in hand, holding off the guards, knowing he would die. "We're going to make it out. We're going to use Mr Park's tunnel."

Min put his hand on her shoulder, squeezing it tight, just as Iseul emerged from the copse. "Warmly sleep-hut. This way."

• • •

Seo lay wedged between Nari and Min, unable to sleep, watching the fire as it fought the wind, expecting to see the barrel of a rifle and the sneer of a guard at any moment. Iseul had found a hollow in the side of a slope, just big enough for them to all squeeze in. At first Min had not wanted to build a fire, afraid that the light would be seen, but as the temperature dropped it became clear they had no choice.

Nari woke at one point, asking where they were, and for a moment Seo thought she must be getting better, but when she reached out and touched her forehead she felt the prickling heat and smelt the sour sweat. She put her arms around her, holding her tight. "I'll get you out of here. I promise."

The sun rose in a haze of orange, a smear on the clouds that stretched the length of the sky. Seo checked the area outside the hollow before crawling out. She crept towards the edge of the copse, her body tense, stopping dead as a bird flew out of a tree in a clatter of feathers, branches and leaves. Seo waited until silence had settled again and made her way to the treeline, looking back the way they had come. The snow lay without a blemish, the fresh fall during the night wiping out their tracks, and she couldn't see any new ones. She leant against a tree in relief – no one had followed them.

The smell made her jerk upright, every sense in her body suddenly alive. She checked the direction of the breeze and followed the smell up the hill, past the hollow and to the top of the rise. The ground fell away sharply, the trees thinning, running down to a small valley. A terraced house with four units sat in the crux, the fields of the small municipal farm spreading away to the north, the boundaries just discernible through the snow. Smoke and steam rose from the chimney of the last unit, carrying with it the unmistakable smell of cooking rice.

Seo flattened herself against the ground, scanning the valley for anyone who may have seen her. Two more rows of terraced houses stood on the far side of the fields, but she couldn't see any sign of the occupants. An almost irresistible urge to run down to the house and take as much rice as she could threatened to overwhelm her. She could feel the hot rice slipping down her throat and she probably wouldn't even mind if they took her back to the camp after that.

The door of the middle house opened, and the sight of the man, an axe in his hand, brought her back to her senses. She watched as he walked, his axe swinging in his hand, around the side of the house and out of sight. One by one the doors opened and the rest of the people emerged, some carrying bundles, others tools, some stopping and greeting each other, before all moving to the far side of the houses and the fields and woods beyond.

It only took a few minutes for Seo to get back to the hollow and explain to Min and Iseul what she wanted to do.

"No, no! The people will snitch. No mush, no meat, back to the camp."

Seo looked at Min. "She needs dry clothes, food and proper warmth for a while. I watched them all go out to work."

Min nodded. "We all need to get out of these uniforms anyway. Someone just has to see us, never mind question us."

Iseul spat on the ground, crossed his arms and turned his back on them, like a child having a sulk.

"You don't have to come," said Seo. "You can wait for us here if you like. But I could smell the white gold cooking…" She crawled back out of the hollow without another a word and had just bent down to gather up Nari's stretcher when Iseul took it.

"I can carry for this shift."

"Thanks, Iseul."

They had no way to hide walking down the valley towards the houses. They tried to crouch as much as they could, but it made pulling the stretcher almost impossible. The houses had seemed so close when they started, but now, no matter how quickly they walked, they didn't seem to get any closer, and Seo thought they would be stuck, walking on the spot, until the people came home and raised the alarm.

They chose the last house, the one Seo had seen the chimney smoke coming from. Iseul reached it first, peeking in through the window before trying the door. They stumbled inside, dragging Nari in, and Seo gasped at the feeling of complete warmth, something she hadn't felt for months. Min went straight to the fire, where a cooking pot dangled on a chain.

"There's rice," he said, his voice hushed in wonder. He took a spoonful and passed it on to Seo. She took a mouthful and then carried the spoon over to Nari.

"Don't try and give her that. She won't be able to swallow it. She needs broth."

It took Seo a moment to process that the voice didn't belong to Min or Iseul.

Iseul pulled a poker from the fire in a shower of sparks and raised it above his head, his face locked in a snarl.

A woman stood in the doorway, the wind ruffling her grey hair. "It's all right," she said, stepping slowly inside, one hand raised in a gesture of reassurance, the other pulling the door closed behind her. "I won't hurt you. If I wanted to do that, I just would have shouted for help."

Seo looked at Min, her mind racing, trying to think of a way out, but she didn't see what choice they had. Min nodded, putting his hand on Iseul's arm, slowly lowering the poker.

The woman smiled. "Thank you." She walked over to Nari. "May I look at her?"

Seo nodded, and the woman knelt down beside Nari, feeling her forehead. "She needs food and warmth." She put her ear against her chest, then raised it with a wave of her hand. "And a wash! Come along, now. Let's get you sorted out."

TWENTY

The woman gently cut Nari's hair, stopping every little while to apply some white powder. It'd take care of the lice, she said. Seo sat on the edge of the bed, watching. She had never known a grandmother but assumed this is what they must be like: gentle but business-like, firm but kind.

The boys had carried Nari through to the bedroom and laid her on the bed, then been banished to the far end of the house. Seo had helped the woman undress her, then watched as she sponged her down with warm, soapy water. She treated the cuts and bruises with an ointment that smelt warm and bitter but stopped at a faint rash on Nari's ribcage.

"Pellagra," said the woman. "I'm not surprised." She turned to Seo. "Do you have a rash?"

"A little," said Seo, instinctively scratching her arm. "Is it dangerous?"

"It can be, if left untreated. But this is very early stages.

You probably all have it." She carried on applying her ointment, peering down at Nari's skin. "If left untreated it will kill you eventually, but it sends you mad first…" She stopped suddenly, as if aware she had said something wrong. "Sorry. Don't be afraid. A few good meals with some meat should do the trick."

"Thank you."

The woman brought some underwear and a shirt, and they managed to get them on her before covering her in a blanket. The material was coarse and scratchy but heavy and warm, and Seo knew her friend hadn't been so comfortable for a very a long time.

Finished, the woman put the bottle of lice powder, ointment and scissors down on the bedside table and opened a small metal tin. She took out a bottle of pills and held it up, staring at them for a moment. "These should still be all right. It's an antibiotic. I was saving it in case I got sick in the winter. But I'm old now…" She gave a short laugh, took out two pills and dropped them into a mug of water, stirring it briskly with a spoon. "Help me lift her head up." She put the mug to Nari's mouth and waited until instinct took over and she began to sip it down. It seemed to take an age, but eventually the cup was empty and they lowered Nari's head back onto the pillow.

The woman hadn't offered her name, and Seo thought it rude to ask, so she simply addressed her with the respect she would show any elder. "Auntie?"

"Yes, child."

"Do you think she'll be all right?"

"I won't lie to you. She's very sick. If the pills are going to help we'll know in the morning. I'm afraid we just have to wait." She went to the wardrobe and pulled out a pair of canvas trousers and a jumper. "These should fit you all right. Can I leave you to wash yourself?"

"Yes, of course."

"Good. Come out when you're done." She clapped her hands, rubbing them together for a second. "Right: let's deal with those boys."

The soap smelt of home, and Seo took her time, sponging away the grime and filth of the camp. Her missing finger made it awkward at times and some of her burn scars still stung a little. Somehow, here, washing herself in the bedroom of a real house, she felt more conscious of her injuries than ever before. She found her hand ugly, something to be hidden away and not talked about, an embarrassing secret.

The clothes Auntie had given her had obviously been made for a boy and hung awkwardly on her body, but they were clean and warm, and made her feel better than she had in months. She sat with Nari for some time after she had dressed, holding her hand in silence. Nari mumbled occasionally, incoherencies that Seo knew were a symptom of the fever. The bottle of pills still sat on the table and she picked it up and read the label. The word '*clarithromycin*' didn't mean anything to her, but she assumed it must be the name of the medicine. "Please work," she whispered, then kissed Nari lightly on the forehead and went out to the other room.

Min sat by the fire, his hair full of lice powder, his face dotted with the ointment, wearing a patched jumper and canvas trousers almost identical to Seo's.

She smiled at him. "I haven't seen you in normal clothes for so long. You look quite handsome." She coughed, suddenly embarrassed, not quite sure why she had said that. A dim wail came from the back of the house, and Seo realised Iseul probably wasn't enjoying his de-lousing. He emerged a few minutes later in a jumper and trousers like the others, scratching at his head, sending a shower of white powder onto his shoulders. He sat down, his face almost completely plastered in the ointment, shifting awkwardly in his clothes. Seo realised it must be the first time he had worn anything that wasn't a camp uniform.

"This one doesn't fit right," he said.

"You'll get used to it," said Seo. "And it will keep you warmer than the camp uniform ever did."

Iseul took a step forward and whispered, "Is this Pyongyang?"

"No. We're not in Pyongyang yet."

"More marching on this shift?"

"No, we can rest for a while."

Iseul let out a sigh, sat down next to the fire with his back to the wall and closed his eyes.

The woman came and sat in a fading maroon armchair placed midway between the door and the fire. For a long time, nobody spoke, Seo steadily becoming more uncomfortable, unsure of what this lady wanted from them or why she had helped them. For the first time, she was able to study the woman's face properly. The lines and wrinkles told her she was old, perhaps the oldest person Seo had met, but they couldn't completely hide the high cheekbones and long, slender neck. She had been beautiful once.

"You are from the camp."

It wasn't a question, and Seo looked at Min, unsure how to respond. She must have recognised the uniforms so there didn't seem much point in lying. But she didn't have to say anything.

"I caught glimpses of light coming from the hill last night and knew someone had lit a fire. There's nothing else out here but us and that camp, so I didn't even have to see you to know where you had come from." The woman reached into the pocket of her cardigan and pulled something out, holding it down in her lap and turning her eyes up towards the ceiling, as if trying to work out what to do. "I was hoping you'd come down. I knew how cold and hungry you must be. There's something I need to ask you, but I'm not sure if I can."

A single tear slipped down the woman's face, finding a path through the lines on her face, as if it had travelled the route many times before.

"It's all right," said Seo. "You've been so kind to us. You can ask us anything you like."

The woman thrust out her hand and Seo reached out and took a small black and white photograph, slightly faded, the edges fraying, but the clear image of a boy about Seo's age smiled up at her.

The woman kept her eyes on her tightly clasped hands. "Did you see this boy in the camp?"

Seo didn't need to look at the photo again to know she had never seen the boy, but something held her back from saying it. "Min, you look," she said, handing him the photograph. "You have a better memory than me."

Min took it, pushing his glasses back up his nose. "I'm…" His voice trailed off.

"It's all right," said Auntie, rising from her chair. "My husband took this nearly thirty years ago now. You wouldn't recognise him." She stood and took the picture from Min, placing it carefully back in her pocket. "I like to keep it close." She turned, steadying herself against the gnarled plank that served as a mantelpiece, and Seo glimpsed the sorrow in her soul, a shadow flickering across her eyes. "I look for him every day on the hill, walking towards me, smiling and waving. When I saw your light..."

Seo turned her face away, her mind suddenly filled with the image of her parents, old and frail, a fading photograph tucked away in a pocket, still waiting after thirty years for her to come back. She wanted to leave, to run all the way back to her town, past the train station, take the shortcut through the municipal farm and bound up the stairs to her apartment. Her mother would be cleaning, her father fixing his chair. She looked at Min, and he turned, holding her eyes, and she knew he was thinking the same.

But it would be suicide. The South would have some way she could get in touch. Surely it was better to know she was alive and safe than see her for a few days and watch her be shot?

"Right: we need to establish a few things." Auntie's voice had taken on its previous business-like tone and it helped Seo to clear her head.

"Most people around here we can trust, but not all of them, so you'll have to stay hidden. The Party don't care about us much; the operation is so small it doesn't yield enough rice for them to really care. So there's no *Immiban* to spy for them, but an agent or two shows their face occasionally, and if that happens we'll have to get you out fast. You're going north, I suppose, to the border with China?"

Min shook his head, dusting his shoulders with lice powder. "We're going south."

Auntie looked at him as if he was cracked. "There's nothing south but barbed wire and land mines."

"We have some… information. It has a high probability of success."

"Then you know something no one else does. But if you're fixed on that, it does make it easier. There's a railway track five miles from here that takes supplies to troops at Musandam and Kijong-Dong. It will shorten your trip by several days."

Seo couldn't help but smile.

• • •

Nari sat on the edge of the bed, doing the buttons on the shirt Auntie had found for her. She stopped and smiled at Seo. "I kept dreaming I was at home."

"I dream of that all the time." Seo went over and buttoned the last one for her, then sat and pulled her friend close. "I was so afraid you'd die."

"Thanks to you, I didn't."

They had been in the house for four days. Nari had responded to the antibiotics better than they could have hoped for. But she was still weak and coughing up green and yellow phlegm. "Better out than in," said Auntie. "Your lungs are expelling the poisons. It's a good sign."

Nari couldn't remember much of their journey from the camp and it hadn't taken long for Seo to fill in the gaps.

"Mr Park?"

Seo let her eyes give the answer. "He saved us."

Nari brought her hands to her face and began to cry. Seo put her arm around her and let her own tears flow, realising that she hadn't allowed herself to mourn for the man who had kept them alive for so long then paid the ultimate price for them to have a chance to get away. The two girls held each other, neither rushing their grief, allowing it to run its course, until Nari wiped her eyes with the back of her hand. "I'm really hungry."

"Then you're in for a treat."

They had eaten well, perhaps better than Seo could remember. Some colour came back to Min's cheeks and his hands didn't seem to shake as much. The new diet had not been easy on Iseul, though, and despite his enthusiasm he had finished several meals doubled over with stomach cramps, his system struggling to process so much rice.

"You mustn't give us so much," said Min. "You won't have enough for the rest of the winter."

"Nonsense," said Auntie. "I only need a few grains to get by."

But they all knew that the longer they stayed the harder it would be for Auntie later. They decided that they would wait two more days for Nari to get as much strength back as possible, then head for the railway and Kijong-Dong.

They spent most of their time sitting or lying on the floor, afraid to go too close to the windows in case someone saw them. Auntie left early in the mornings, coming back at lunchtime, then staying out again until dusk. Occasionally Seo risked a peek out of the window, her curiosity winning over her caution. She found it hard to determine what the people did all day. She saw them moving around in the fields or coming out of the woods with logs or bundles of food, but they were all things that shouldn't take all day. The fields lay barren and frozen solid, so they couldn't do anything with them until spring. Sometimes she felt as if she was watching a story, the people acting out a day's work, filling the time in the only way they knew how.

The morning before they had planned to leave, the door burst open and Auntie rushed in, her hand on her chest, trying to slow her breathing.

"They've come. Time to go."

"What is it?" said Min. "What's happened?"

"The authorities are here. I don't know if it's a random check or if they've come from the camp, but they are checking all the houses and will be here soon."

"But what—"

"No time for questions! Let's go!"

Seo felt four days of comfort swept away in an instant. They had stayed too long, and now danger hunted them again.

It only took them a minute to gather up their things and get to the back of the house, Iseul beating them all to the window.

"Now, you know the route?" said Auntie.

"We know." Seo took a step forward, and before Auntie could object threw her arms around her. Min and Nari did the same, holding her tight. She pushed them gently away, holding out a thick cylinder. "It's a torch," she said. "It works by dynamo. Just wind the handle at the bottom."

Seo took it and shoved it into her pocket. "Thank you so much," said Seo. "I don't know how I can ever repay you."

"Don't get caught."

They heard the sound of a fist hammering on a door a little way up and an incoherent shout.

"Go, children," she said, pushing them away. "I hope you find your way in Kijong-Dong."

They skirted the field, Seo keeping next to Nari, making sure she didn't fall behind. Three men stood in the middle of the field, wrapped up against the cold. One of them glanced in the direction of the group of friends and Seo winced, ready to sprint, expecting a shout. But the man took the shoulder of the one next to him, pointing at something in the opposite direction, and no one else noticed as they reached the treeline and stopped a few feet beyond. Seo whispered thanks to the anonymous man and looked back towards the buildings. She could just make out Auntie's house, a thin stream of smoke curling out of the chimney. A truck, one of the Black Crows used to take people to the camps, squatted on the hill, its tyres half buried in the snow.

"Come on, Seo," said Min. "We can't waste any time."

"I never found out her name. Why did I never ask her name?"

"It's Won. She had written it on the back of the photo."

Seo felt Min's hand tugging at her sleeve, took one last look at Auntie Won's house, turned and fled into the woods.

TWENTY-ONE

They had watched the railway line for two days and not a single train had passed. The sun rose slowly, turning the clear winter sky from grey to red to orange, lighting the deserted stretch of track where they had set up camp to watch and wait. Iseul had found another quiet and sheltered spot for them, but already the cold had crept back into Seo's body, and with every mouthful of dried rat she longed to be sitting on the floor in Auntie Won's, a hot bowl of rice in her hands.

Iseul busied himself collecting wood they didn't need, or grass and bark they couldn't cook, as uncomfortable doing nothing as he was in his new clothes. He had somehow managed to hang on to his old uniform and wore it underneath the jumper and canvas trousers, going about the day as he would have done in the camp, perhaps afraid he wouldn't get anything to eat if he didn't.

"Here," said Seo, passing Nari a strip of meat.

"No, thanks."

Seo just held it there, fixing Nari with what she hoped was a stern look.

"Fine." Nari snatched it and took a bite, chewing quickly.

"You need your strength."

"I feel much better, and I don't like sitting around not helping."

"There's nothing to do."

Seo looked at her friend. Her lips had regained some of their colour and her eyes didn't seem so clouded anymore. But she had developed tiny lines at the far edge of each eye, like the ones her mother had, only smaller, fainter. Seo wondered if they would go in time, or would always be there, like her scars and the stump of her finger, permanent reminders of pain.

"Quick, get your stuff!" Min appeared at the camp, his face flush from running. "I think I can hear one."

It only took them a moment to gather up their few possessions, and they half stumbled, half slid through the snow towards the tracks. They stopped in a shallow ditch just a few feet from the rails that Min had camouflaged with branches. Iseul tugged at Seo's sleeve. "Now we are marching to Pyongyang?"

"It depends if we can get on."

"Get on?"

"Shhh…"

At first Seo could only hear the breeze as it ruffled the leaves on the branches, then the unmistakable sound of a train growing louder until it became the only thing they could hear.

"It's going slowly," said Min.

"How do you know?"

"The rhythm of the wheels over the tracks. And the fact we haven't seen it yet."

"Wait until the cab has gone past, then if we see a truck we can get on we'll go together. But all together! All right?"

Min and Nari nodded just as the train came into sight, the diesel engine coughing out fumes from an exhaust on the roof. Even from a distance, Seo could see the driver, and she pushed herself closer to the ground. Min had been right: it seemed to creep along, groaning with the effort, slowly enough for them to jump on if they got the chance. If someone saw them they had Nam's coat as a bribe, but they would pretend to be orphans, which she knew from experience no one really cared about anyway.

The engine rolled past, the driver's attention straight ahead. The second carriage held a few soldiers, some sleeping, the others chatting quietly, but that seemed to be the only passenger car, the next two cargo trucks, the contents sealed behind locked doors.

"The last one," said Min. "Get ready…"

"Let's go," said Seo.

The sliding doors of the cargo carriage had been left open on both sides, the light shining into an empty interior. Despite how slowly the train appeared to move, once alongside it Seo had to sprint to keep up. Behind her Nari began to wheeze and she looked back to see her face flush and her eyes wide.

"You first, Nari! Grab the rail – there's a step just beneath the door."

Nari flung her arm out, gripping the rail, the train seeming to pull her along for a moment, then she got one foot onto the step and hauled herself up, collapsing onto the floor and gasping for breath. Seo followed, turning as soon as she got on board and offering her hand to Min, then Iseul, and they all fell to the floor, gasping in air.

Seo lay facing the ceiling, then turned her head, slowly taking in her surroundings, her body jarring in time with the sound of the train on the tracks. The carriage was as empty as it had looked from the outside, probably emptied at a stop further up the line. It stretched some distance away from the doors in either direction, the light not reaching the farthest corners, leaving them hidden in darkness.

Nari lay next to her, struggling to catch her breath, but gave a thumbs-up when Seo asked if she was all right. Min had already got up, watching the countryside as it drifted past outside. Iseul sat with his back to the wall, staring straight ahead, hands wrapped around his knees, and it took Seo a moment to realise he was frightened. She got up and walked over to him, steadying herself as the train lurched around a corner, the axels groaning with the strain. She squatted down in front of him. "Are you all right?"

He dropped his eyes, staring at the floor. "This thing is not normal. My belly feels all upside down."

He had never seen a train, thought Seo. Of course he hadn't. "It's all right." She rested her hand on his arm. "It's just a like a big truck, you know, like the ones in the camp."

"A big truck?"

"That's right."

Iseul lifted his eyes and looked around a little. "This one could fit a hundred crushers!"

Seo smiled, but before she could reply, Iseul gripped her wrist and held a finger to his lips. Seo immediately signalled to Min and Nari, straining her ears for whatever sound Iseul had heard. At first she couldn't make out anything except the noises of the train, then slowly, almost imperceptible at first, she could hear someone snoring. Her heart froze, and she looked around, trying to find out where it could be coming from. Iseul poked his finger towards the opposite corner and she nodded.

Min pulled the dynamo torch from his bag and they crawled towards the corner, the snoring becoming more distinct with each inch. Min cranked up the torch and pointed the light on the edge of the shadow, slowing making its way further in, revealing boots, then army trousers and a battered coat. He lay so still that if it wasn't for the snoring, Seo could have believed he was dead. An empty bottle lay by his head, another full one standing next to it, the smell of corn liquor hanging in the air like a gas.

Min switched off the torch and they crawled back a little.

"We have to get off," said Nari. "He's a soldier."

"He's unconscious," said Seo.

"I saw a man like that once," said Min. "He collapsed outside our apartment. No matter what we did, we couldn't wake him up."

"But he will wake up eventually." Nari rubbed her hands together, anxiety growing in her eyes.

Min flashed the torch into the corner, checking every inch. "He's not wearing a gun and there's no sign of one."

"Do we have anything we can tie him up with?" asked Seo.

"We've still got some strips of shirt left."

She gave him a jab with her foot, but he didn't even stir, his snoring continuing its gentle rhythm. "Good. I think he's going to be useful."

They pulled him out into the light by his feet, but even then it took several more prods from Seo before he showed any signs of waking. He lifted his head up, muttered something incoherent and let it fall back to the floor with a thud. This seemed to be the jolt he needed, and he opened his eyes, his face straining with the effort. He caught sight of the empty bottle still lying on the floor and made to reach for it, trying to separate his hands in confusion until the realisation hit him that he had been tied up.

"What is this… What's happened… How…"

His eyes darted about before settling on Min. "Thieves! Help!" He tried to use his legs to push himself away but couldn't find any grip. "Help! I've been tied up…"

"Quiet!" shouted Seo. "We won't hurt you and the others are too far away to hear you anyway."

The soldier squinted at Seo, as if trying to get her into focus. "You're just a child?" He let out a noise that sounded halfway between a cough and a laugh. "I've been tied up by bloody orphans." He spat on the floor, leaving a dribble down his chin. "You do know you sparrows are flying the wrong way? This train goes to the border. Nothing down there for you but a bullet."

"You've ridden this train before?"

"Of course I have. I used to be stationed down there…" His voice trailed off and he began searching the area around him, twisting his head and body around. "There was…"

"Is this what you're looking for?" Seo held up the bottle of corn liquor and gave it a shake, the liquid catching the light.

"That's mine…"

"Why are you back here?" said Nari. "Why aren't you with the others?"

"Give me the bottle."

"Answer the question."

Anger flashed across the man's eyes, his hands began to shake and, despite the cold, a bead of sweat ran down his forehead. He took a deep breath, as if trying to calm himself. "Because I got drunk. Apparently the others don't like my singing and always send me back here to sober up. What they don't know is I always keep a supply back here." He reached out his hands, the trembling increasing, the anger in his eyes replaced with imploring.

Seo looked at Min, he nodded and she held out the bottle to the soldier. He forced himself into a sitting position, managed to grip the bottle with both hands and took a long swig, keeping his eyes closed as he swallowed, a dribble running from the corner of his mouth. Seo took the bottle back, placing it carefully on the ground, just out of the guard's reach. He opened his eyes, colour back in his cheeks and his hands steady.

"Thank you," he said. "Always need a little something when I wake up to keep the tremors away." He wiped his mouth on his sleeve, then held out his hands. "Could you untie my hands?"

Nari laughed. "You must think we're stupid."

"You're heading south on a train without a travel pass towards the most heavily guarded area in Korea. I sure as hell don't think you're smart. But there's four of you and one of me, my legs will still be tied, and I need to pee."

Seo thought about it for a while. "Iseul, stand behind him. Make sure he doesn't try anything."

"There's a knife in my back pocket. Be easier to cut it."

Seo signalled to Iseul and he pulled out a small pocket

knife, handing it to Seo, who turned it over in her hands. It had a wood and steel handle, the blade kept sharp and the name '*Ji Woo*' engraved along one side. "Your daughter."

"My wife."

Seo cut the twine, and Min and Iseul flanked him as he shuffled to the side of the carriage and peed out the door with a deep groan of relief. He sat back down and asked for another drink, but Seo refused.

"The knife then. Please, it's very important."

"You can have it when we get off." She handed it to Min, who slipped it into his pocket. "I promise."

The soldier grunted and spat on the floor. "A sparrow's promise."

Nari picked up the bottle of liquor and handed it to him. "You can trust us."

He took the bottle, slowly, cautiously, as if unsure why she would give it to him. He took a long swig, screwing up his face as he swallowed. "So, where are you getting off?"

"That's what you're going to tell us."

• • •

Iseul stood by the door, his position for the last hour, a grin stretching across his face. He stuck his arm out, then his leg, and finally his face, letting the wind from the train wash over him for a moment, before pulling himself back in and falling to his knees with laughter. "I'm like the birds in the sky!"

The soldier alternated between swigging from his bottle and falling asleep. They had to keep waking him up to ensure they didn't miss their spot. He had laughed when they told him they wanted to get off at Kijong-Dong, but Seo had put this down to drink and ignored him. Min and Nari sat back to back, chatting occasionally but mostly silent. Seo sat slightly away from them, keeping an eye on the soldier and trying to suppress an increasing sense of anxiety.

They had no more food left and spring was still some way off. If Mr Park's tunnel had gone, or if they couldn't find it, they had nowhere to go, and she was pretty sure that they wouldn't put up with orphans in a place like Kijong-Dong. It'll be all right, she told herself; they would get out.

She gave the soldier a nudge and he jerked awake.

"Well?"

He looked out, then pulled himself to his feet, hopping a few steps towards the door. "Nearly. You should get ready."

Within a minute they all stood by the door, the soldier pointing out towards a low hill. "You see the flagpole?"

Min leaned towards the door. "What flagpole?"

"There, on the horizon."

"That can't be a flagpole. To see it from here it must be huge."

"It is. Listen: head towards the flag. Kijong-Dong is between it and the hills. But..."

"What?" said Seo. "What is it?"

"Look, I've never been there, but I've heard it's not what they say it is."

"I've heard that too."

Min handed him back his knife and he took it with a smile. "Thank you. I need this."

"Ready," said Nari.

"Don't forget to start running as soon as you hit the ground, otherwise you'll fall flat on your face."

Despite his warning and their best efforts, not one of them

managed to stay on their feet, tumbling along the scrub at the side of the tracks like a handful of chopsticks. Seo picked herself up, tentatively stretched her arm to reassure herself it wasn't broken and looked back at the train. The soldier leant out of the door, one hand gripping the side, the other waving in long, slow arcs. Seo waved back, waiting until he had faded from sight, before turning and facing the hills.

. . .

They all lay on their bellies, staring out in the darkness. The clouds had smothered the moon, leaving the countryside inked in shades of black. But after the trek up the hill, Seo welcomed the cover of night. The going had been fairly easy, but they had never been more aware of the presence of people: the sound of an engine in the distance, an answered shout. the smell of woodsmoke on the breeze. Then it had all vanished, as if they had crossed some invisible border, replaced with warning signs painted with the silhouettes of soldiers shooting intruders and 'KEEP OUT' written in screaming letters.

The sun had set long before they reached the crest of the hill, and after waiting so long to see it, dreaming of being able to visit, she could only imagine what Kijong-Dong looked like.

"It's strange," whispered Min. "I thought there would be some lights at least."

"Perhaps we're in the wrong place," said Nari.

She had barely finished speaking when dozens of lights blinked into life below her, as if the owners of a hundred apartments had decided to switch them on simultaneously.

"Wow, that was weird." Nari looked at Min, as if hoping for an explanation.

"Maybe the lights are on timers?"

Iseul poked Seo in the side. "Is that Pyongyang?"

"Nearly, we're almost there. Just one more shift."

Min took out the map that Old Man Park had given them, unfolding it in front of him. He stared at the map and then at the lights below, his finger matching drawings to buildings. "The building is next to a radio antenna, but I can't see that in the dark. I think it must be on the left. I don't think it has any lights on, which I really hope means there is nobody in it."

They all stared down at the yellow and white glows for a moment. "Ready?" asked Min.

But suddenly Seo wasn't sure if she was. What if they were caught? What if Park's tunnel wasn't there or it had been filled in long ago? Perhaps there were orphans in Kijong-Dong and they could live by the railway, stealing and scavenging whatever they could? But they were too old; they would be rounded up by the police or the army, probably sent back to a camp, and she knew she couldn't bare that. Not for herself, not for her friends.

"I hope they just shoot us."

"What?" said Nari, and Seo realised she had murmured the words out loud.

"Nothing." She reached out and took her friend's hand, holding it tight. "Come on, we'd better get going."

The buildings slowly came into view as they walked in a crouch down the snow-patched ground towards the town. The clouds shifted, and by the moonlight Seo could make out the famous blue roofs stretching off into the distance, the sight of them giving Seo a new feeling of hope.

Iseul stopped, his hand outstretched, and everyone else automatically did the same, dropping to a crouch.

"What is it?" whispered Seo.

Iseul squatted down, his arms resting on his knees, his face turned slightly up, staying perfectly still for a moment before answering. "I can't hear-snitch. No workers, no crushers. Whole world sounds dead-dead."

Seo turned to Min. "What do you think?"

"Maybe it's not so strange. There might be a town meeting somewhere. Perhaps self-criticism?"

"Let's keep going," said Nari. "We can't stay out here on the hill."

It only took a few more minutes to reach the first building and they flattened themselves against the wall. Seo took a deep breath and poked her head around the corner. A narrow track led between rows of terraced houses, some with lights on and some without, but still throwing out enough light to be seen. She edged around the corner, keeping her body flat against the wall, shuffling her way along, when the wall suddenly vanished and she felt herself falling backwards, her feet in the air, before landing heavily on the ground.

"Seo!"

She sprang to her feet, looking quickly around, trying to understand what had happened. She stood inside the row of houses she had been walking around, but instead of furniture, walls and curtains, there was nothing but dust and empty space; it didn't even have dividing walls. She looked up and saw a cloud pass across the face of the moon.

Min's face appeared at the window she had fallen through. "Are you all right?"

"Fine," said Seo, picking herself up from the ground. "Why isn't it finished?"

"You better come out."

Seo walked through the gap where a door should be and across to the building opposite. Iseul squatted on an empty window frame, his arms folded, his face wrinkled into a scowl, which gave him the look of a grumpy old man. "This world is cold and empty. No mush, no fire."

Seo walked quickly to the nearest house that had a light. But it was nothing more than a shell, like all the others, a single bulb screwed into a socket on a wall. She stared at it, as if she had never seen one before, trying to piece together in her mind what had happened to the town. Min tugged at her sleeve and they made their way along the deserted street, not bothering to hide anymore, listening to the wind moaning in the empty houses.

As they moved further on, towards where they knew the border lay, the buildings became better finished. Some had doors and window frames, and one three-storey block of flats had a few pieces of furniture on the ground floor, but the armchair looked filthy and threadbare, and the round dining table stained and rotten. If anyone had lived there they had left years ago.

"This is it?" said Nari, turning on her heel, her arms wide. "This is the great Kijong-Dong? This is the place everybody dreams of?"

"I don't understand..." But as soon as the words were out of her mouth she realised the truth: this was what Kijong-Dong had always been, what her world had always been.

"COMRADES OF THE SOUTH!"

The voice exploded out of the darkness, almost knocking Seo off her feet. The others instinctively flattened themselves on the ground, Seo searching for the source.

"YOU LIVE UNDER THE REPRESSION OF THE IMPERIALISTS AND THEIR PUPPET GOVERNMENT! THROW DOWN YOUR WEAPONS AND BE WELCOMED INTO THE REPUBLIC AS BROTHERS AND SISTERS!"

Min pointed upwards and Seo looked up to see an enormous speaker fastened to the wall at the top of the block of flats. It looked similar to the ones on the top of the Information Vans, but at least ten times the size.

Min gestured for them to move and they half walked, half ran back the way they had come. As soon as they were behind the speaker the volume dropped and it wasn't long until they were able to talk again.

"Do you think they can hear that in the South?" asked Seo.

"I think that could be the point," said Nari, her hands still over her ears. "And I thought the Information Van was bad."

"We need to get moving," said Min, pulling Park's map from his pocket. "There may not be anyone living here, but being this close to the border, there will be patrols."

Min checked the map and they headed off in the direction of the building Park had marked out. After the warning about the guards, they moved cautiously again, keeping to the side of the buildings, avoiding any with lights. The propaganda speakers kept yelling at the South, and somehow it made Seo feel more vulnerable, as if any minute it would shout for them to halt and surrender.

*"ALL ARE EQUAL IN OUR GLORIOUS REPUBLIC!
BREAK FREE FROM THE SHACKLES OF
CAPITALISM!"*

Min gestured for them to stop and Seo moved closer. He stared at the map for a moment then pointed at a building on the other side of the street, a metal antenna pointing to the sky like a giant tripod. "I think that's it."

Seo looked at it for a moment. All her hopes lay inside a squat, two-storey lump of concrete, its metal door left slightly ajar. "All right. Let's go."

*"CITIZENS ENJOY A REWARDING AND HEALTHY LIFE,
SUPPORTED BY OUR PHILOSOPHY OF COMPLETE
SELF-RELIANCE!"*

They ran across the street and through the door, Seo holding it open for the others. She glanced back at Kijong-Dong, city of dust, and stepped through the door just as a guard came into sight at the end of the street.

*"WE PROVIDE FOR ALL! NO COMRADE IS LEFT IN THE
COLD!"*

Seo pushed the door shut as quietly as she could, not knowing if he had seen her or not. Her shaking hands found a bolt and it slid into place with a creak and a shower of rust. She slowly took two steps back and felt Nari's hand grip hers. She didn't need to tell them what had happened. The building had no ceiling, and in the light of the night sky she watched the door handle drop slowly down with a steady screech of metal on metal. It stayed there for a moment, then crept back to its starting position. Seo held her breath, counting the seconds, every fibre of her being willing the guard to turn and walk away.

The bang of a fist on the door made Nari gasp, and Seo felt her hand tighten on hers. The guard shouted out, demanding to know who was inside, then he began shouting for back-up, whether into a radio or just into the distance Seo couldn't tell, but it took only a few seconds for him to be answered by the slow crescendo of a siren.

"Let's go!" said Seo.

"It's the far back corner," shouted Min.

At first, they could see nothing as they scrambled to clear away the dust, earth and leaves, only the cold grey of the concrete floor. The hammering on the door became louder and Seo knew it was only a matter of time before more guards arrived and they knocked it down. Please, Mr Park, let it be here.

"ALL KOREANS MUST BE FREE! WE ARE ONE NATION DIVIDED ONLY BY THE CRUEL HATRED OF THE AMERICANS AND THEIR ALLIES!"

"Here!"

Seo rushed over to where Nari had grasped a thick metal ring. She took hold, heaving with all her strength, but her missing finger made it difficult to grip and pain shot up through her hand. Iseul pushed her away and together with Min and Nari they pulled, the veins bulging on their necks. At first nothing happened, then slowly a section of the floor began to rise, only a centimetre at a time at first, then quicker, until it flew open, sending them flying backwards onto the floor.

Min shone the torch and Seo saw a ladder bolted to the side of a circular shaft vanishing into blackness below. Iseul clapped his hands and made to climb onto the ladder, but Min grabbed him. "Wait. We don't know how long this has been closed. We need to let some air get in there."

The door shook, rattling in its frame.

"I think I'll risk it," said Nari. She put her foot on the first rung and began to climb down, Iseul only seconds behind.

"You go, Seo," said Min. "I need to see if it will close."

Seo began the descent, stopping a few feet down to watch Min. A metal rod hung on a hinge on the underside of the door, and Min reached out and grabbed it, pulling the door closed as he came down.

"ONLY BY EMBRACING THE WAYS OF JUCHE CAN WE DETERMINE OUR OWN DES—"

The world snapped into silence and darkness, the ladder vanishing in front of Seo's eyes.

"Are you all right, Min?" asked Seo.

"Fine. There's a bolt to lock the hatch, but I don't think it will hold anyone for long."

"Let's go then."

At the bottom, Min pulled out the torch. They stood at the bottom of a concrete shaft about twenty feet deep and six feet wide. The air hung thick around them, smelling of decay, and Seo struggled to take it in; it was like trying to breathe compost. Nari began to cough.

Min examined the walls; the counterweights that helped

to open the hatch hung on one side, the other sloping down out of sight under an archway. Above it a fading yellow sign read 'ESCAPE ROUTE 7'.

Iseul spat on the ground, pointing towards the tunnel. "Cannot go this way. The air is wintry. No breathing, no marching."

Seo knew he was right and turned to Min. "It was built to be used. There must be something…"

Min scanned the walls with the torch, stopping at a point about two feet from the ground. He knelt down and Seo heard the thump of a large switch being pushed down. A bulb flickered above their heads for a moment before holding and a row of strip lights blinked into life down the tunnel and out of sight. At the same time a deep rumble came from somewhere in the wall and Seo felt air rushing over her face, stale and dusty at first, then blowing clear, like a night breeze. She lifted her face, her eyes closed. "I love you, Mr Park."

"We're not there yet," said Min.

The tunnel had been laid smooth and even, most of the lights still working, and they made good progress. It flattened out after about ten minutes of walking, but Seo couldn't tell how deep they had gone. Every twenty-five metres or so a fan had been attached to the ceiling, designed to suck air in and blow it further down the tunnel, but despite that the further they went, the fouler the air became.

Seo lost track of time, and when the lights ran out, she wasn't sure how long they had been walking. The ceiling ended suddenly, like it had been sliced off, the smell of concrete replaced by damp earth. Min shone the light forward, and they slowed their pace, walking with care. Like Mr Park had said, the tunnel had not been finished, and Seo could see the wooden supports and boarded walls and ceiling. When the lights stopped so did the fans, and it took only a few minutes before they all started struggling for breath. Nari suffered the most, her cough becoming almost constant.

"Stop," said Seo. "We have to rest for a moment."

Nari slumped down against the wall. "I'll be all right," she said, each word punctuated by a gasp for breath.

"We can't wait long," said Min, looking back over his shoulder. "They must be in the tunnel by now."

Seo put her arms under Nari's shoulders and pulled her up. "Come on. It can't be much further."

They stumbled along, half carrying, half pulling Nari, Min's torch just a tiny circle of white in the dark, until they collapsed together on the ground.

Seo tried to pick Nari up again, but she waved her away. "No good."

Even in the poor light of the torch Seo could see the effort it took for Nari to talk.

"No air. You go."

"No way. We're so close."

"Crushers!"

Seo looked down the tunnel and saw a distant torch beam fluttering between the wall and ceiling.

"You need time," said Min, thrusting the torch into Seo's hands.

"We don't have any."

"I'm going to make some. Point the torch up at the ceiling."

Seo did as she was told without thinking, the thought of the guards dragging them back through the tunnel blocking out anything else. The light caught one of the crossbeams sagging under the weight of the earth above it, the boards that formed the ceiling cracked and leaking earth.

"Hold it there," said Min. He vanished into darkness for a moment and returned carrying a rock. In the distance Seo heard voices, almost inaudible, but she knew they must have seen her light.

The torch began to flicker, lighting Min in a series of snapshots, like photographs taken with a flash: Min shaking the support. Min leaning back with the rock in his hand. The rock smashing into the support and the sudden realisation of what he was doing.

"No, no, no, no… *Min!*"

A wave of dirt and dust washed over her with the sound of a building collapsing. She felt arms tugging at her and reached out for Nari. Then she ran, the darkness engulfing her, her eyes and mouth full of earth. She felt someone beside her and tried to call out, but no sound would come. Then metal in her hands. Something falling on her head. Starlight and air.

She stumbled on, the wind on her face, the cold earth scratching at her hands and knees. She looked around, desperate to see Nari or Iseul, but she could see nothing, not even sure which way she had come. She fell to the ground, knowing she had lost. Her friends lay buried in the tunnel, a grave she had dug for them with her plans. She tried to cry out, but no sound would come.

"Freeze! Don't move!" The soldier walked slowly towards her, his rifle raised. "Who are you? Identify yourself!"

Seo spoke, pleading with the soldier to spare her friends. Help me find them, she said, and you can take us all back to the camp, just let me know they are alive.

The soldier stared at her. "I said identify yourself!"

She began to speak again, slowly realising that though her mouth moved no words came out. She grabbed her throat, straining as hard as she could, trying to squeeze out some sound, but none came and she knew her voice had gone, buried somewhere deep under the earth with her friends, where she could never find it again. She let her body roll down onto the ground, pulled her legs up under her and longed for darkness to carry her away.

Orientation Visit Record

Days Since Arrest:	35
Location:	Beyond the Perimeter Fence (City)
Subject:	Jane Doe (Possibly Ra Eun Seo)
Age:	Unknown (Estimated at 14)
Origin:	Suspected Defector from North Korea
Medical Condition:	Evidence of severe physical trauma
	Evidence of Post-Traumatic Stress Disorder
	Inability to speak
Supervising Officer:	Kim Soo Jung

X – *Do you recognise any of these buildings?*

SUBJECT DOES NOT WRITE OR SIGN.

X – *I don't think you've been here before. But I think this is where you were trying to get to. Wasn't it?*

SUBJECT DOES NOT WRITE OR SIGN.
X – *Can you tell me the name of this city?*

SUBJECT DOES NOT WRITE OR SIGN.

X – *You don't seem to believe me no matter what I say, what I show you.*

SUBJECT DOES NOT WRITE OR SIGN.

X – *OK. This isn't working. Let's head back. We'll have to try something else.*

Returned to Institute: 13:35

TWENTY-TWO

The room had a view of a single tree and the top of the fence. On clear days the sky became a brilliant blue, stretching on forever, and a bird would sit in one of the branches of the tree and sing. Seo wondered if it sang for anyone in particular, perhaps its mate, but no reply ever came, so it would preen its feathers then fly quickly away.

They had put a small desk in front of the window and Seo spent some of the day writing the things she knew they wanted to hear about. They kept telling her that everything was all right now; she was safe and no one would hurt her. But she couldn't shake the thought that it was all a trick, a show put on to make her think she had made it to the South before they pulled back the curtain to reveal the cage in the clearing with Mr Chi's body still swaying gently on the rope. So she wrote her confession, as detailed as she could. She saw no point hiding anything from them anymore.

Two days before they had taken her in a van and showed

her more lights and buildings and people and cars than she had ever seen: a kaleidoscope of sound and colour as if one of the stories from *Blossoms on the Moon* or *Long Road Home* had come to life in front of her. It's Seoul, they said, and it was hard not to believe them, but she tried because she didn't want it to be true. Min, Nari and Iseul were dead or back in the camp, and whether through a bullet or a ride in the Crow, she just wanted to be with them.

They called the place she stayed at the Institute for Assimilation, and Seo didn't know what that meant and never asked. They kept the door open and every so often someone would poke their head around and ask if she needed anything. She never did. A woman with a striped apron brought her meals on a tray: hot rice and meat with kimchi and soup, or dumplings with noodles. She found it hard to eat, and often the woman who brought the tray would stay with her to make sure she ate as much as she could, before taking the tray away again.

Sometimes they set her work to do. That day she taught herself how to convert from the *Juche* calendar to something they called the Gregorian one. She knew it was the year of *Juche* 106, meaning 106 years after the birth of the Great Commander. Mr Chi had always taught her that the rest of the world (except the Americans, of course) had adopted the *Juche* calendar out of reverence, so perhaps it was a test to see if she already knew how to do it. She completed the formula and came up with the number 2018. She looked at it and did the sum again, but it seemed to be right. As far as the Americans were concerned it was two thousand and eighteen years from the beginning of what they called the Common Era, or Ano Domini, which seemed to be linked to the birth of a god.

The trembling began in her legs, as it always did when she became stressed or confused. Soo Jung had taught her how to control it and she closed her eyes, slowly spelling out the word '*calm*' in her mind, stopping and going back if the fear interrupted her, ensuring each pen stroke of the characters shone as clear as if they were written on paper.

"Are you ready, Seo?"

Seo opened her eyes to see Soo Jung, the woman who always asked her the questions, standing in the doorway. She only seemed to own two dresses, one dark blue and the other purple. She wore the purple one today, and that always seemed to mean she had something new to show her or tell her. Her slightly chubby face always wore a smile and her voice reminded her of Auntie Won, although she must have been at least twenty years younger.

"Are you all right? What's wrong?"

Seo tapped her forefinger against her temple, the sign they had agreed to use to show she was confused.

Soo Jung picked up the paper she had been working on. "But this is right. You've done really well."

Seo stuck her thumb in the air to show she understood.

Soo Jung sat down on the bed and patted the space next to her. Seo sat, her hands on her knees, waiting for the instructions for the day.

Soo Jung took a deep breath. "OK…"

OK. Seo still found the phrase Soo Jung used so often confusing at times. It seemed to have several meanings: *Everything is all right. Do you understand? That's good!* Or *I need to tell you something…* Judging by the look on her face today, she needed to tell her something.

"You've been here a long time now, Seo. Forty-seven days,

to be precise. And I've got permission to tell you something."
She paused, scratching the tip of her nose. She's nervous,
thought Seo. "But I'm worried. I still don't think you really
believe what we tell you, even after we took you into the city."

Seo pointed to herself, then touched her lips, before
making a large circle in the air with her right hand. *I believe
everything.*

Soo Jung smiled. "You're a clever young woman, Ra Eun
Seo. But you don't fool me. Which is why I'm going to show
you, not tell you." She stood. "Come on."

They walked together along the corridor towards the
room she always sat in and wrote answers down on the
notepad. But instead of stopping and going inside they
walked straight past.

Seo tugged on Soo Jung's sleeve and waggled a finger in
the air. *Where are we going?*

Soo Jung didn't answer at first and walked on in silence
for a while, before stopping abruptly at a white door. She
turned to face Seo, her eyes covered with a thin film of
tears. "You're going to think I'm very cruel. But you have to
understand that not everyone who comes here is who they
say they are and your circumstances were… well, unusual to
say the least."

For the first time since crawling out of the tunnel Seo
felt peace returning to her. This is it, she thought. This was
the moment they would tell her it had been a trick and she
would walk through the door to a scaffold or a Crow. She
would miss Soo Jung. She hadn't realised until that moment
that she had formed a strong bond with her interviewer. She
had always been kind and Seo hoped she wouldn't get in too
much trouble for that.

Soo Jung turned and looked at the door. "We are sure now that you are who you say you are. Or who've you've written you are, I should say. Normally we wouldn't do things this way, but you never believe anything I say, so I think this is the only way. Please don't hate me for too long."

In her head, Seo said, "I don't hate you at all," and gently touched her face.

Soo Jung took her fingers and held them against her cheek. "I hope that voice comes back. I think this might do it, which is why I haven't taught you real sign language. I don't want you to rely on it. I want to hear you sing." She turned, opened the door and Seo walked through.

She found herself in a long white room, with rows of tables and chairs. Sunlight shone through windows that took up almost the entire length of the walls. She could see the tree that stood outside her window and the fence beyond. At first she didn't understand what was happening, turning back to Soo Jung, her hands raised in a question. Soo Jung pointed to the far corner.

Min sat on a chair, gazing out at the lawn and the trees, one arm in a sling. Nari sat next to him, examining the nails on her right hand. Min looked up and his eyes met Seo's. He nudged Nari, and for what seemed an age none of them moved, the room filling with a silence Seo could feel. She took one step forward, then another, her legs trembling, her cheeks already soaked with tears. Min and Nari stood together, walking slowly towards her, then faster, then running, meeting in a muddle of hugs, cries, laughter and tears.

TWENTY-THREE

That day, holding my friends tight, I found my voice again. It came slowly at first, a few words before any complete sentences, something familiar but strange, like finding out you did have to learn to ride a bicycle again after all.

At first, I kept writing in the third person, pretending Ra Eun Seo was someone else and not me, but slowly, almost in time with my voice retuning, I replaced 'she' with 'I' and 'her' with 'my', and gently settled back into my own body.

Nari had been the first one they pulled out of the tunnel, conscious but struggling to breathe. They found Iseul further in, lying half-covered by the pile of earth that had buried Min and allowed us all to escape. They had both persuaded the soldiers to go back in and dig Min out. He had managed to avoid the main brunt of the cave-in, which had spread behind him rather than forward, and they found him unconscious, his left arm broken but otherwise unhurt.

Soo Jung needn't have worried; I didn't hate her for a second. And she had been right: if she'd just told me they were alive, I wouldn't have believed her. Mr Park's tunnel made the news after someone at the institute leaked the story. The North claimed the Americans had dug it as part of their invasion plans, but Soo Jung had told me it was probably one of several escape routes for the leaders in case they had to flee. I'm glad Mr Park's tunnel was famous for a while. He would have liked that.

We spent our days in lessons, sometimes alone, sometimes together. We did the usual school ones like maths and Korean, and others that helped us understand our new world and how to live in it: managing money, using a washing machine, ordering coffee or shopping for groceries in stores stocked wall to wall with every food stuff imaginable – and quite a few I couldn't have imagined. We each found our own way through them, managing some better than others. For Min, the hardest thing had been the Internet. He sat at the computer, the teacher guiding him through web pages and search engines, showing him how to find information and sort out the most valuable. After an hour he had got up without a word and walked quickly out of the room. I followed him and found him standing in the corridor, staring off into the distance, his eyes filled with anger and a deep sadness.

"There's so much, Seo," he said, his voice quiet and tight. "I never dreamt there was so much to know. Why do they hide it all from us?" He took off his glasses and wiped his eyes. "How *dare* they hide it from us?"

It's the only time I've seen him cry.

For me, it was the news that the North had started the

Korean War. I think I had still clung to the hope that not everything I'd been raised to know was a lie, that at least the regime that had moulded me from birth had been born of defence, not attack. But it wasn't true. The Great Commander had invaded the South, been driven back by the United Nations forces led by the Americans, and only saved from destruction by the intervention of the Chinese. The Americans had refused to use nuclear weapons, so it had ended as a stalemate, each country back where they had started.

The sense that she had betrayed her father still haunted Nari. She had regular sessions with a doctor and had begun to accept that it wasn't her fault, but it had left her spirit frail. The first time we rode the subway in Seoul, the crowds and noise had left her frozen in terror. Soo Jung had to take her to a park to find some calm and peace.

It was a long time before they let me see Iseul. Soo Jung said he was struggling to assimilate to his new life and kept trying to escape. We had all found it hard, especially our first trips to Seoul; the noise and lights and mass of people could be overwhelming. I couldn't imagine what it had been like for Iseul.

When I eventually saw him for the first time I went alone. Min and Nari had lessons to attend, but I didn't want to put it off any longer, worried he would feel abandoned, so had persisted until Soo Jung had spoken to whomever she needed to speak to, and finally persuaded them it would be all right.

He sat at a table in the room I met the others in, the tall glass windows framing a picture of the first signs of spring. The room seemed even whiter than I had remembered it and

I caught a faint smell of disinfectant. He didn't see me at first and I watched him for a while, suddenly aware that I cared for him as much as Nari and Min.

He stood when he saw me, a smile spreading across his face, and I ran quickly over, my arms wide. He hugged me tight, patting my back. "I'm so glad you're here."

"It's wonderful to see you." I tried to swallow the lump that grew in my throat, fighting the tears.

He took a step back, straightening his shirt a little. "I'm very pleased to see you," he said, as if reciting lines from a script. "Please have a seat." He went to sit down, then immediately stood again, indicating that I should sit before finally sitting himself. I knew he must have been practising how to behave and did my best to hide my smile.

He seemed the same, but if I'd seen him on the street I might not have recognised him. Someone had cut his hair and parted it to the side, but strands stuck out at angles all over his head, as if refusing to be tamed. His face had filled out, and it made him look younger, perhaps not much older than me. But the change ran deeper than that and I couldn't say at first what it was.

A jug of water sat on the table with two glasses and he poured us each one, taking a small sip and placing it down in front of him. I broke the silence by asking him how he was and what he had been doing. He spoke about the lessons he took: language, speech therapy, learning to write and the practical things we had all done. He hadn't been allowed out of the institute yet, and listened, his mouth hanging open, to my stories of our trips to Seoul.

"Even better than Pyongyang?"

"Much better than Pyongyang."

He began to tell me about his day-to-day life, concentrating hard, using vocabulary I hadn't heard from him before, forming complete sentences slowly and deliberately. He slipped up sometimes and this seemed to upset him. As he spoke his voice became tighter, tears appearing at the bottom of his eyes until it became a struggle for him to even get a word out.

I reached out and took his hand. "It's all right, Iseul."

His head fell onto his arm as he finally let go, his body shaking with sobs. I put my arm around him, not knowing whether to speak or stay silent. A door opened at the far side of the room and a man in jeans and a blue shirt stepped into the room. "Can I help?" he said.

"He'll be all right. Can you leave him with me for a while?"

The man took a moment to make up his mind before nodding. "I'll be right out here if you need me."

We sat without talking, Iseul slowly bringing his tears under control.

"I'm sorry, I'm very shameful."

"There's no shame in crying, Iseul. We've all done it."

He wiped his eyes on his sleeve. "Not for crying. For… I can't belong here."

"Don't say that!" I grabbed his arm, gripping it tightly. "Of course you do. Think of what we went through to get here."

"Everything feels wrong. Even this chair. It's too…" He shifted his weight in the seat, his face rumpled into a frown.

"Then let's sit on the floor." I took his hand and sat down cross-legged. Iseul squatted down next to me, his arms resting on his knees, suddenly looking more like himself again.

"It gets easier, Iseul. We've all found it hard. The noise, the crowds, using money, trying to understand why we've been lied to all these years, kept prisoner for so long."

Iseul turned his faced away and for a moment I thought he would break down again, but he took a long breath in, forcing his tears away. "It's not that as much. It's…" He tapped his chest. "It's inside of me."

"What do you mean?"

"All the time in the camp, just think about mush – meals, I mean – and how to snitch, how to get more mush, more rest, only for me. I was never thinking about anything else. Never to help someone."

"That's not true," I said, leaning forward, putting my hand on his arm again. "You helped us all to get out. We probably couldn't have done it without you."

"But I didn't do it for you. I did it to get nice meals with meat. Not to help." He turned his head and stared out of the window. "Here it is different. No one will like someone like me here. Someone who is not helpful."

I couldn't hold back my own tears any longer as I witnessed the final atrocity from the camp. "It's not you, Iseul, it's them. You're a good person, I know you are. Don't you remember that night when I was in the cage? You brought me soup because you were worried I was cold. Not just because you wanted something. You said it was 'upside down.'"

He nodded at the memory.

"Then you touched my hair and told me it would be all right. It was one of the kindest things anyone has ever done for me."

He managed a smile, but I could still see the conflict in his eyes.

"We all did things we would never do outside a place like that. You did what you had to do or you would have died. Don't let them make you think it's your fault."

"But I know I am not good, because all they want to do is change me: speak this way, eat that way, don't do this, do that."

"That's not trying to change you. That's just to help you fit in when you leave. We've all had to do that."

He looked at me, his head cocked slightly to one side. "Even you?"

"Even me. We're not so different, Iseul. The camp I grew up in was bigger than yours, that's all. You're a good person, one of the best I've ever met. Better than any of those crushers, any of those 'leaders.'"

"Better than Hwan!" said Iseul, strength returning to his voice. "Better than Nam!" He turned, pulling his head back to spit, catching himself just in time, so it looked like he had just gagged on something. "Sorry." He wiped his chin. "Sometimes I forget."

"You wouldn't be you if you didn't spit when you mentioned that name. Just do it outside, maybe."

He smiled, some warmth returning to his face. "I don't have to change everything."

"You can't change everything. We are who we are. And I'll always like you."

We sat in silence for a while, staring out of the windows at the sunshine in our new world. I couldn't help thinking how difficult things would be for him, but it was hard not be filled with hope. The worst part was over.

"What time is it?" Iseul jumped up, as if he suddenly remembered something.

"You've got a watch," I said, pointing to the red strap on his wrist.

"Too troublesome," he said. "Quarter this, after that. No need. If it's time to eat, the crushers – I mean the helpers – said you could stay and have some too!"

"I'd love to." I held his eye, a smile growing on my face. "What are we having?"

He lifted his hands and we clapped in unison: "Warmly mush with meat!"

TWENTY-FOUR

Nari sets the flower in the freshly dug hole, pulling and pushing the earth in around it, patting it down gently, as if she is a putting a baby to bed. She's let her hair grow almost to the length it used to be but always keeps it in a tight ponytail when she's working in the garden. I kneel next to her, handing her flowers from a small pallet, enjoying the last of the day's sun on my face as we slowly move down the flowerbed. Out of the corner of my eye I catch a glimpse of a figure moving quickly towards us.

"Here he comes," I whisper.

"I don't want to talk to him."

"He's just trying to be friendly."

"Shhhh…"

"Hi, Seo!"

"Oh, hi, Chul. I didn't see you there," I say, in what I hope sounds as throwaway as possible.

"Nice evening."

"Yes, it is."

Chul taps his foot, looking around, taking his hands out of his pockets, then sticking them back in again. I smile and nod, glancing at Nari, trying to will her to say something.

"Hi, Nari."

I look at her, the seconds of silence ticking over in my head, but just before I decide to nudge her she speaks.

"Hi. I'm afraid I'm a little busy."

"Sure, sorry to disturb you, it's just…" He glances at me, and I turn away, pretending to count the flowers still left on the pallet. He lowers his voice a little. "I was wondering if you'd like to go for a walk after dinner tonight? You know… just maybe chat and stuff…"

Another silence, and this time I don't want to nudge her; I want to hit her.

Nari sits back on her heels and looks up at him, shielding her eyes slightly from the sun. "Maybe."

"Umm… Great. I think."

I stop pretending to count flowers and glare at Nari – *maybe!*

"I'll see you then," he says, looking like someone who's found a ten thousand-won note but is beginning to suspect it might be fake.

I watch him go, scratching his short, spiked hair, his right foot curling in a little with every step. He had been beaten by his foster parents and I often wondered if it was an injury or if he had always walked like that. He's lived in Seoul all his life, moving from foster home to foster home, until being brought to the Farm. Its real name is the Choe Centre for Youth Wellbeing, named after the couple who founded it and still run it, but their sprawling site about forty-five minutes outside of Seoul earned it the nickname and it stuck.

Eight of us share the four bedrooms, two in each. Nari and I are together and Min shares with Chul. We're the only ones from the North; the others, like Chul, have all been in foster homes before coming to the Farm. It's friendly and comfortable, although most people stay on their own quite a lot. The main house has a large common room with a pool table, darts board, couches and a large radio, although I think Nari, Min and I are the only ones who ever turn it on. TV is restricted to the weekends.

Nari fell in love with the place immediately. Still scared by the noise and rush of Seoul, it offered peace and a chance to be away from the city. Mrs Choe showed her how to look after the gardens, delighted to have such an eager student, and you could always find Nari weeding a flowerbed or examining a shrub – tending to her 'children'.

Min wouldn't mind where he was, as long as he had access to the Internet, spending most of his free time absorbing all the knowledge he could find. Mr and Mrs Choe have started to limit how much time he spends on the computers, insisting he gets some fresh air now and again.

Nari lets herself fall backwards, her arms in the air, her trowel dangling from its strap on her wrist. "I don't want to go."

"You need to make friends."

"I've got you, Min and Iseul."

"Other friends. Don't get me wrong, I love you. But Soo Jung says we need to make friends who are from here to help us fit in more. You know that."

Nari pulls herself up and takes off her gloves. "It's hard."

"I know, but he really likes you. It's written all over his face."

"He won't for long, not when he finds out—"

I take her hand in both of mine and stare into her eyes. "Don't say that. That's not true."

She turns her face away.

"I'll come with you if you like."

"Really?" She thinks about this for a moment. "OK then, I'll go. But only if you come."

"I promise."

She stands. "Come on. Dinner will be ready soon."

Min appears at the door. "Come on, guys. Food."

"Coming!" Nari takes a step then stops, her right hand trembling, the movement slowly spreading through her arm as the terror builds.

I jump to my feet and put my arm around her, holding her tight. "You're safe. I'm here. You're safe. Breathe." I shift position, lifting her head up so I could look her in the eyes. "Spell it out after me: C-A-L-M."

It takes Nari five attempts before she can spell the word without having to stop and start again, her trembling slowly subsiding and her breathing returning to normal. She sits down slowly, letting her head drop between her knees. "It's all right. I'm OK."

"That one went pretty quickly," I said, kneeling down next to her. "It's getting better."

Nari nods, but I know how hard it still is for her and the main reason she shuns other people's company. We sit in silence until she feels strong enough to get up. "Are you coming or having a chat first?"

"A quick chat. I won't be long. Are you all right?"

Nari nods and walks off towards the house, leaving me sitting on the grass, the sun sitting just above the trees. For some reason I always think about my parents in the evening: my mother in her battered hat, my father beckoning to me with his half-finger. Something deep down tells me they are still alive. I can't explain it exactly, but if they died I think I would know, would be able to feel it somehow. Min feels the same about his mum, but Nari still won't talk about her father, her guilt a large factor in her paralysing bouts of fear.

Nari calls them my 'chats', when I sit in the evening before dinner and tell my parents my news, like how I finally found my song, the one we listened to the first day we found the radio. Soo Jung had taken us into Seoul to teach us how to order a burger at a fast-food restaurant and we walked past a music store that had it on through a loudspeaker. I stood, transfixed on the pavement, suddenly back on that hill with Min and Nari, as people went around me, giving me funny looks. It's called 'At Last' by Etta James. It's really old, and the woman in the shop told me that not many people listen to it anymore, especially not people my age, but somehow that made it even more special, like it's still my secret and I'm the only one who knows the tune. From Etta James I moved on to Nina Simone, Muddy Waters and Janis Joplin, then Amy Winehouse, Adele, Taeyeon, Ailee, Coldplay, Eminem, G-Dragon, Taylor Swift and PSY – a range of music I couldn't have imagined existed. But I couldn't get angry or upset, as Min had about the Internet. I'm just glad to be able to have it my life now. I told them about Min and how he wants to be a teacher, to share the knowledge of the world with others. And Nari, with her plans to work in the countryside, maybe for one of the National Parks, spending her days with nature, the school we go to and our trips back to the institute to see Soo Jung. She keeps telling us that we need 'closure', which will help us to fully adjust. But I don't want to close anything; I want it wide open. I don't want to hide my hand with its missing finger, or my burns when I go for a swim. These are things that are part of me and shouldn't be locked away.

I told them about the night we met Iseul in the restaurant before he headed off on a speaking tour to raise awareness about the North. We had a cake with candles and balloons, and he looked well and happy. I think he'll be fine, and he's promised to be in touch as soon as he's back.

I haven't told them about my feelings for Min yet. Looking back, I think I always loved him, since we were very young, but never really understood it. I know he feels the same, but we haven't said anything to each other yet. The time will come soon, though, and I'll take his hand on a walk by the river, knowing he'll never let go.

Tonight I tell them about my audition for the School of Performing Arts in Seoul. I'm going to sing 'At Last' (in English) and 'Try' by Park Ji-min. The nerves wake me up at night sometimes, but nothing would stop me going through with it. I can dream of being a singer again, of a future with music and beauty and wonder.

I hear another shout coming from the doorway and stand, knowing I can't stay any longer. The walk takes me past the trees and shrubs we planted shortly after we arrived: a rose bush for Auntie Won, jasmine for the soldier from the train, willow for Mr Chi and, in the middle of the lawn, an oak tree for Mr Park, which I always stop and touch, impatient to see it fully grown. The Choes have promised that as long as they own the land, they will never be moved or taken away, and I believe them.

The sun has dipped just below the trees, sending spears of light flying through the branches, looking almost tangible in the evening sky. I reach out, trying to touch them, to feel their warmth, to pluck one from the air to keep in my pocket so I'll never know darkness again.

"Come on, Seo!"

"OK!"

I say goodbye to my parents and turn, heading towards the house, where steaming bowls of noodles sit on the table, Min and Nari are waiting, and the radio is on.

Acknowledgements

Many thanks to Joanna Devereaux and Maurice Lyon for their invaluable notes on early drafts of the book. To my wonderful wife Niamh, whose support and encouragement was so valuable. To all the defectors, whose courage has done so much to enlighten the world about the true nature of life in the DPRK. And to K&S: I pray you are safe.

Author's Note

Whenever I had mentioned North Korea (or the Democratic People's Republic of Korea, to give it its formal title) I was met with raised eyebrows, hurried responses and the occasional finger tapped against the temple: *it's crazy there, the people are different, they don't think like us, they don't know anything...* Admittedly, knowledge is strictly controlled, but the rest is complete nonsense.

After seventeen years in Southeast Asia, I had become fascinated by this isolated, unlit country, and had promised myself that before I left the region I would go. At the time, travellers could only access North Korea by air from China, Russia and Malaysia, or take a train from Dandong. As the national airline of the DPRK is the only one to receive a one-star rating from Skytrax, I chose to stay on the ground.

Visitors to North Korea are strictly controlled and I was shown a few select parts of Pyongyang, including numerous monuments to the leaders, by two charming, nervous guides, their often flawed or false knowledge of the world nailed into them by a regime who don't dare let its population know the truth.

My trip lasted four days, and I left tired and depressed, eager to get out, to leave the cold, empty streets, the artless propaganda and the vicious cruelty of its government far behind. Then a girl singing in a cold, dark school room and another gathering water from a stream by the railway tracks as my train hurried me back to China created the first glimpse of the character I would call Ra Eun Seo.

Writing outside one's own cultural or ethnic background has become highly controversial. Authors who do so are often met with accusations of cultural appropriation. These accusations raise important questions about the nature of fiction and truth, as well as cultural identity and ownership, and possible answers are beyond the scope of this brief note. As I have lived most of my life outside of my country of birth, married a 'foreigner' and have children with dual nationality, I can't speak with any great confidence about what my cultural identity might be. But regardless of how people identify, it has always struck me as sinister that, for example, a young Ugandan author who wants to write a novel set in Canada must seek permission first. From whom? Surely, she is free to write as she pleases.

Whatever the current thinking on social media might be about these matters, this is not a book about culture. To suggest that the current regime in North Korea is a result of Korean culture strikes me as a great insult. The oppression of the people there is no more their own fault than the Russians under Stalin or the Cambodians under Pol Pot.

This is a book about our inhumanity to others. In particular, to our children who we condemn to a life of conflict and ignorance when we tell them what to think and who to kneel before. For this reason I have kept direct reference to culture to a minimum, but where necessary I have done my utmost to ensure they are accurate. If I have made mistakes, I would be very pleased to be corrected.

I have not taken any characters or events from true stories. The world of Seo and her friends is a fictional one. But I believe it is also a plausible one, approached as I try to approach all my writing: with humility, respect and an ever-growing belief in our common humanity.

On my last day in North Korea, as I walked away from the demilitarised zone after hearing a demonstrably false account of the Korean War, one of my guides fell into step next to me:

"What do you think about Western people, Harry. The Americans?"

I hesitated, worried it might be a trick, and tried to think of the answer she would want to hear. She looked earnest, though, so I answered truthfully:

"I think they are the same as everybody, the same as you and me. They want peace and safety. I think they want to be free and happy."

"Yes," she said. "That's what I think. That's what I hope."

Thank you for your interest in my work.

Best wishes,

Harry
Mauritius, June 2022

Milton Keynes UK
Ingram Content Group UK Ltd.
UKHW020936041023
429879UK00012B/95

9 781805 140498